The Complete Ballet

Also by John Haskell

Out of My Skin
American Purgatorio
I Am Not Jackson Pollock

THE COMPLETE BALLET

A Fictional Essay in Five Acts

John Haskell

A Public Space Book

GRAYWOLF PRESS

This publication is made possible, in part, by the voters of Minnesota through a Minnesota State Arts Board Operating Support grant, thanks to a legislative appropriation from the arts and cultural heritage fund, and a grant from the Wells Fargo Foundation. Significant support has also been provided by the National Endowment for the Arts, Target, the McKnight Foundation, the Lannan Foundation, the Amazon Literary Partnership, and other generous contributions from foundations, corporations, and individuals. To these organizations and individuals we offer our heartfelt thanks.

Published by Graywolf Press
250 Third Avenue North, Suite 600
Minneapolis, Minnesota 55401

www.graywolfpress.org

Published in the United States of America

ISBN 978-1-55597-787-0

2 4 6 8 9 7 5 3 1
First Graywolf Printing, 2017

Library of Congress Control Number: 2017930113

Cover design: Kapo Ng

Cover art: Shutterstock

For my daughter

We die daily. Happy those who daily come to life as well.

GEORGE MACDONALD

The Complete Ballet

ACT ONE
La Sylphide

The story of my ballet begins in a large house. It has wooden beams, a stone fireplace, and in front of the fireplace a man, slumped in a wingback chair, is sleeping. He's young, about to be married, still living with his mother, and we can't know for sure but he's probably dreaming, not about his future wife but about another woman, in this case a girl, a young girl, a thin, young ballerina playing the role of a sylph.

When I say *the story of my ballet* I'm referring to what they call Romantic ballet. And I say *begins* because at a certain point ballet changed. What it was, a court dance, became what it is, a way of moving in the world and thinking about the world and it started around 1832. That's when Marie Taglioni first performed the ballet *La Sylphide*. She was the Sylph, and the Sylph was a kind of angel, and because angels can hover above the ground that's what she did. Arnold Haskell, the ballet critic, said of Taglioni that *she walked among the tree tops*, meaning that when she rose up on the points of her toes she seemed to be blown about, like a feather. And I mean literally blown about like a feather. As James exhales, she's blown away from him, and when he inhales she's pulled toward him, drawn by his breath and by her curiosity, about love and desire and about sexuality, her own sexuality, which is why she's come to the house of this . . . and yes, James is handsome. He's physically perfect. His strong, erect torso, and the muscles of his calves and hamstrings, stretching the leotard under his kilt, are attracting the Sylph, his stalker, or really she's more like a bee hovering around his sleeping body, her own body covered in layers of thin, white fabric.

The story of my ballet started years ago when my daughter was about three years old. She saw a production of *The Nutcracker*, and because she wanted to be like the girl in the story I began reading her the story, and then other ballet stories, and the books we had described the lives of the characters she loved, Odette and Giselle and although they suffered, and usually died in the end, my daughter started imitating them. She called herself Aurora or Clara, and wearing Halloween butterfly wings she danced around the house in a way she thought a sylph would dance. Her infatuation with ballerinas got me interested not just in ballerinas but in the roles they played, in their lives and lovers and here I am, years later, thinking about the father of the original Sylph. Filippo Taglioni was the choreographer of *La Sylphide*, the one who taught Marie the footwork that made her famous, the footwork she dedicated her life to. It's the footwork we now think of when we think of classical ballet but for the audiences who first saw her dancing en pointe it must have been a revelation. Here was someone, without ropes or harnesses, leaving the gravitational constraint of the earth, rising up to what they believed was up there, which was heaven. They didn't see the years of subjugation, the hours spent molding the muscles of her legs and feet, the bruises, the pain, the laces of her slippers tied so tight the blood stopped flowing. What people saw when they saw her was a vision, part girl and part creature, an ethereal creature who, flying across the stage, balancing literally on the tips of her toes, reflected their ideas of what an ideal person could be. All ballet is about idealization, and in Romantic ballet the bodies of the dancers don't just dance. By taking on the attributes of actual people they become actual human beings, and every human has a story, and we live in our story, and by following the choreography of that story, step by step, our lives are created.

La Sylphide is set in Scotland, the land of fairies and spirits, and because James is Scottish, it wouldn't be unreasonable to assume he believes in the reality of sylphs. But he doesn't. Like a lot of people he only believes what he already knows, and when he encounters an actual sylph, the white tulle cascading out from her waist, he assumes she's a dream. Because the wings attached to her back, the gossamer wings, allow her to fly, and she does fly, something humans can't do, she must be a dream. *His* dream, because she's hovering around *his* chair. And being a dream, although he can feel the heat of her body passing up through the hairs of his nostrils, it takes a while before he believes it. Plus there's the fact that no one else can see her. His old friend Gurn, his only friend, is snoring away by the fire, and even if he wasn't sleeping he wouldn't see her because sylphs can be invisible to those they're not *flirting* with, and although flirting isn't the right word, the girl is interested in James.

I don't remember the first ballet I ever saw but I remember the ballerina. She was only slightly older than I was, and what I remember wasn't her dress or her dancing but her nakedness. I was about fourteen, and innocent, and because her costume was meant to suggest her nakedness, it did. Even now when I watch the videos of dancers from the Kirov or the Royal Ballet, I can sometimes imagine them without their costumes, just bodies moving, and I can begin to imagine what people saw when they saw Taglioni for the first time. Before her, ballerinas danced in gowns, like wedding gowns, but Taglioni, because she wanted people to see what her feet and her ankles were doing, raised the hems of the dresses she wore. And in 1832, to expose your ankles was saying, in effect, look at my body, and what does my body inspire? She was tacitly acknowledging the sexual aspect of her personality, and she could let that sexuality emerge because of the ethereality of the character she was playing. *Ethereal* is defined as being delicate and light in a way that seems too perfect for this world, and because she embodied the purity and asexuality of a nymph or a sprite or a spirit, she could get away with more revealing costumes.

In *La Sylphide*, as in any Romantic ballet, a woman, or a fantasy of a woman, is the star of the show. Her dilemma, usually, is that she's going to die, or *is* dead, and the question arises: Is love still possible? And how do you get to a place where love is possible? When the Sylph alights, coming down off her toes and kneeling over James, asleep in his chair, her innocence is being tested. *Innocence* originally meant *not injuring*, and she knows it's dangerous, stretching the confines of what her life has been so far but she's tempted. She can feel the desire to reach across the arm of the chair and touch his ribs, and below them his soft belly, rising and falling, and she's tempted because it's new to her, and also because it's forbidden. She looks across the room to Gurn, snoring away under his wiry red beard, and we assume he's asleep. James is also asleep, and she leans over him, feeling his warm breath and the warmth of his body radiating into her skin and the pores of her skin, and she's not rubbing against him but she imagines what rubbing would be. And it's not a typical temptation because he's not the one who's tempting her. It's her own desire, pulling her closer to him, to an experience of life and the desire of life, and that's when she places her two lips, which had been hovering over him, on his two lips, and by opening *her* lips she opens *his* lips and that's the kiss, when James wakes up, he remembers.

But was it real? Immediately James rouses his friend, wanting to know if what he felt, or saw, or thinks he saw, or was I dreaming? But Gurn doesn't know what James might have seen because he was dreaming his own dream, not about a sylph but about Effie, the young woman James is going to marry. So he doesn't say anything. Partly he's guilty for dreaming about his friend's fiancée, and partly he's jealous that she's not *his* fiancée. And James isn't listening anyway. He's having trouble explaining the kiss because he's still trying to register the kiss. Like a dream in which you have to pee, and then waking up, you find you really *do* have to pee. Which means the dream is not necessarily not real. James is feeling the kiss and feeling the dream of the kiss, and the dream and the actual kiss start to merge, like two tangential ideas that, when they come together exert a force that works its way from the nerves in his lips, up into his brain, and from there it works its way down his body, like a current, where it pools in his pelvis. When he asks his friend about the vision he thinks he saw, about a girl leaning over him and touching him, Gurn looks up from whatever he was pretending to distract himself with. In ballet, everything is either danced or acted out in gesture, and when Gurn acts out his answer James is unsatisfied. Some creature made contact with him, a girl, and he looks toward the fireplace where she seems to have disappeared, and you didn't see it? I definitely saw . . . and he doesn't know what he saw, and Gurn reminds him that he's about to get married, that it's normal to have some premarital anxiety and he needs to get it together, *it* meaning his emotions, which are wild, and *getting it together* means control, which in his case means denial.

Ballet, at some level, is about the tension between, or the union of, control and abandon. Dance originated as a way to speak with the gods, to celebrate and plead, and to act out the Dionysian urge to abandon our bodies to some greater force. And the history of dance has been a history of taming that force, of joining the orgiastic impulse with an impulse that would give it structure. Control is part of it, and molding the body into an idealized version of who we want to be is also part of it. Which is why the Sylph appears to be part of this world, but also part of another world, a mythic world. It's why she straddles not only the binary notions of human and nonhuman but also of man and woman. She's not quite one or the other because, first of all, she's not fully formed. She's virginal, with the androgynous attributes of someone who's been poisoned or cursed or enchanted to remain always a virgin, always in search of love but never able to consummate that love. And the men who fall in love with her are not completely normal either. James, normally, would be thinking about his fiancée, excited and nervous, but it's hard to focus on her right now because his attention has turned to the air, to a creature, asexual and therefore supersexual, imaginary and therefore perfect, who has kissed him. And because he's a dancer, and because dancers are attuned to the irrationality that resides in the body, and because the nature of dance is to follow the dictates of the body, the dichotomy of real and imaginary becomes elastic.

Today we do not know how the great Taglioni danced—from the prints and lithographs we can only recognize the incorporeal effect she produced on her contemporaries—but her art is not dead. Some little girl in London, Paris, or Milan dances differently because Taglioni once existed. She will carry part of Taglioni in her, as only an exciting memory, but a memory that is creative, that has made and still is making dancers who will possess something of her poetry, even some of her technique, and especially the will to serve.

—ARNOLD HASKELL

Unlike Haskell, I'm not interested in writing a guide to dance. I'm trying to find for myself a version of life that expresses itself like dancing, like the moving body thinking itself into existence. Not being a dancer I don't understand all the intricacies of a bourrée or pas de chat, and partly because I don't, when I watch a ballet, or a video of a ballet, what I see in the story is a version of life that's enough like mine but different, not necessarily better but yes, in a way, more beautiful and meaningful and we all have desires. Like any myth a great ballet expresses both my desires and the afflictions that follow. Like anyone, Effie and Gurn and James, and even the mother wants the world to be different. Which means they want themselves to be different. And this affliction, in the story, seems plausible. It wasn't uncommon, in that particular Scottish village, for a son to live with his mother. And the mother, interested in her future daughter-in-law, has been upstairs with Effie, hemming dresses and lacing up slippers, and when Effie walks down the stairs she's glowing. James doesn't notice, but Gurn does. When Effie steps off the final step he bows to her, a little awkwardly because, never having been in love he doesn't know how to act. But he tries. He presents her with a basket, not of flowers, but he's been hunting, and the basket he offers her has a bird inside. Effie looks in the basket, and although it's weird to give someone a bird, a dead bird, in the version by the Bolshoi Ballet, Effie kindly accepts his awkwardness. She's more interested in the man she's about to marry, and when she turns, reaching out with her hands, signaling her desire for attention, because James is distracted by thoughts of the Sylph he can only manage a distracted smile. And I suppose it's because she's preoccupied with marriage preparations but she doesn't notice, when he takes her hands, that his attention is only a pretense of attention. Hi, honey, he seems to say, and by giving her an affectionate hug he convinces her that his love is undiminished. He says he loves her, and he wants to love her, and Gurn is seething but what can he do?

The wings we see, sprouting like wings on the back of the Sylph, are not completely imaginary. I say *sprouting like wings* because, although in productions of *La Sylphide* the feathers were sewn into pieces of fabric, and the fabric was held together with wire, in the story of *La Sylphide* the wings seem to actually exist. And they do. We all have them, vestiges of what birds have, and what angels have, and I speak with a certain authority because years ago, after my marriage fell apart and I moved to Los Angeles, one of the things I did was touch people's bodies. I called myself a masseur, or sometimes a massage therapist, but really I wasn't anything. I'd taken a class in Swedish massage at a so-called academy in Hollywood. I studied pressure points and basic anatomy, and by the time I graduated I'd learned enough to begin seeing clients. I called them clients, but because I was still learning about bodies, and my hands needed to experience a lot of bodies to know what any one particular body needed, I offered my services free of charge. I had another job, an evening job that paid me money, and through this other job I came to know Cosmo. He was an acquaintance who became very quickly a friend, an older man who introduced me to a part of Los Angeles I never would have known. Because he was a businessman he had access to what was called a Xerox machine, and with his help I printed up flyers, pieces of paper I stapled to telephone poles with my number written on tabs that people could tear off. I had a portable massage table which I would set up in my living room, and although I didn't have many clients I had some, and one of them was a woman in her midthirties, with back problems. I'd seen her once before, which was encouraging, the fact that she'd returned. I had alleviated some of her symptoms, meaning some of her pain, and when she lay on my table now, on her stomach, her bra unhooked, I lifted her red cotton shirt up to her neck so I could see her scapula. I pulled her stretchy pants down to the crack of her buttocks so I could both see, and work with, her entire spine, the sacral part and the cervical part and her problem was tension. Whether it was mental or physical, or probably a combination, what I tried to do was to get the muscles around her spine to expand. I rubbed my hands together with aromatic oil, getting them hot, and I would use the heat in my hands to dissolve whatever was knotted up in her. When a muscle tightens, the muscles surrounding it, thinking there must be a reason for tightening, also begin tightening, imitating the first muscle. My job was to tell them to relax, that what they thought they were supposed to be doing wasn't helping, and the trick was to tell them very gently. If you try to force a muscle to relax it usually rebels, which causes more tightening, and the technique I was taught was to find whatever muscle was causing the most tension and press down hard enough on that muscle to wake it up. That's a metaphor, obviously, but in a way muscles are like human beings, they don't like to wake up, which is why I used the weight of my entire body, pressing down into the big gluteus and the little gluteus, trying to get into the fascia surrounding the obturator and piriformis, and because we're mostly unaware of these deeper muscles they're sensitive. They don't like change. Which is why I kept pressing, almost to the point of pain, using that pain to locate and release the source of this woman's tension. I used my thumb, and sometimes my elbow, and muscles have a job to do, to move bones, and when they're asked to do a different job, that's when tension arises, and the beauty of massage is that the effects are instantaneous. Not always, but in this case, once I removed the pressure, not only did I see the relaxation radiating into the woman's skin, I heard her moan, a moan signifying liberation from pain, and then I moved my fingers up her back, to the place where her wings would have been. The latissimus muscle runs up from the sacrum, spiraling around the kidneys, upward and outward to its attachment at the upper arm. It's a sheath, covering the scapula and the muscles that connect the upper back and the arm, and this is where our vestigial wings attach. What I tried to do with the woman was create in her flesh the idea of something like a pair of wings, rising from her spine, into her back ribs, following the course of her serratus muscles and rising around her cervical spine to lift her head. Ballerinas carry their heads, not in front of them like most of us, but directly over the spinal column. And because changing alignment in one part of the body requires changing other parts, my work was to wake up the woman's armpit, which was part of her collarbone, which was part of her neck and skull and when I finished my work, and when she sat up on the table, her face was relaxed. I hadn't touched her face but the tension around her mouth had softened and her arms dangled off her back. And when she stood up off the table and got dressed I gave her some stretching instructions. Letting go doesn't just happen. The information about who we are is stored in our muscles, and because muscles are elastic they tend to return to the familiar.

The choreography of the original *La Sylphide* was lost when Filippo Taglioni died. The dance we have now was made by August Bournonville, a Dane, a few years later. It has different music and different dancing but the story takes place in the same grand Adirondack-style lodge, with chairs and tables, a gigantic fireplace, and the bridesmaids have gathered around the bride-to-be. Effie, in her twirling dress, is charming and intelligent, and once she's received her wedding gifts she joins the corps de ballet in a joyful dance of a girl becoming a woman. During her solo she lifts her arms, extending her leg in a graceful développé that expresses the sense of stepping into the newness of an expanding future. Effie has seen what can happen between a man and a woman, what happened between her mother and father, and she's determined not to let that happen to her, to live instead a life of love and understanding, and she's happily dancing with her friends when Madge appears. James, standing at the edge of the party, doesn't notice the old witch because he's looking for the Sylph, scanning the air for the image he remembers, and he thinks it's her sitting beside the fireplace but it's Madge. And a witch is the opposite of a sylph. Madge has a walking stick, few teeth, knotted gray hair, and in ballet performances she's often played by a man. And partly what frightens James is her genderlessness. He doesn't acknowledge his fright because that would be unmanly, and he takes the idea of manliness very seriously. Whatever fear she arouses in him, instead of feeling it, he turns it into anger. He's heard about the old woman, that she's basically harmless, probably insane, but he can't help feeling a repugnance that borders on hate, and he doesn't ask himself the source of that hate, which is in him, he just attacks her. Verbally at first. You hag, he says. You ugly old hag. You disgusting, ugly . . . He wants to hurt her feelings but she doesn't seem to have any feelings, and his friends try to calm him down.

Joseph Cornell was an artist, born in 1903, on Christmas Eve. He was sometimes called a Surrealist but he never attached himself to a school or style. He was a collagist, piecing together old magazine photos and postcards, bits of glass, dime-store jewelry, beads, marbles, fabric, and his most famous objects were the boxes he made. In them he told the story, obliquely, of loss and unrequited love, and he had a fascination with the Romantic ballerinas. Marie Taglioni, Fanny Cerrito, Fanny Elssler, Carlotta Grisi, they all had boxes either dedicated to them or inspired by them. He had a basement studio in a house he shared with his mother and invalid brother in Queens, New York, on a street called Utopia Parkway. His days were spent in Manhattan, selling fabric, and at night he sorted and arranged and tended to his collection of cultural detritus, bits of the world forgotten by the world, and he especially liked mementos of young ballerinas. In some ways he lived like a hermit, holed up in his crowded studio, but he also liked to get out into the world, taking long lunch breaks to walk the streets of Manhattan. He stopped at junk stores and secondhand stores, and it's natural that he felt an affinity with the Romantic ballet, and especially with the ballerinas who danced it. We can't ever know what happened in his mind but in his art he had a crush on them, on their youth and grace, and their nebulous sexuality made them interesting. Their unattainability made it possible to desire them without having to deal with them, and the series of boxes he made, titled *Homages to the Romantic Ballet*, is a meditation on ethereality and ephemerality, and however much he lived in this world of nostalgia, he seemed to never lack friends. And through one of these friends he met a ballerina from his own time, Tamara Toumanova. She'd been called a baby ballerina, but by the time Cornell met her, at an art opening, she was already twenty-one years old. Cornell was forty-seven, and I think he probably expected her to view him as what he looked like, a once handsome, now shrunken man, poor, troubled, possibly asexual. But she admired him. She liked to have conversations with him, and possibly the conversations were one-sided, her talking and him listening, but they started spending time together. She invited him to visit her dressing room and he was happy to oblige. He became a regular there, sometimes presenting her with drawings he'd made, or sometimes he'd bring her an intricate box, incorporating the story of the ballet she was dancing. Later, he got the nerve to ask her, if it would be possible, to give him a button from her costume.

Effie is good at signaling her desire, and at the party, when she signals her desire for attention, James can read what she wants. And he wants to comply. Inasmuch as he knows what love is, he loves her. He's heard about what love is supposed to feel like and wishes he felt it more than he did, but when she extends her hand he takes it, dutifully. The guests all gather around, talking or dancing, not necessarily paying attention to Effie and James but James is aware of them, in his peripheral vision, watching him. He tries to assume the look of affection, trying to focus on Effie, and when she presents her cheek to him, a soft part of her but not a private part, he knows what he's supposed to do, and when his lips touch the skin of her skin, that's when he thinks he sees, in the corner of his eye, the Sylph. His heart skips a beat, but when he turns it's only Madge, the ancient and ageless witch. She's dipping a tea bag into her cup, a tea bag filled with herbs and weeds that probably keep her alive, but just barely, and bitter steam is rising from the lip of the cup. Being a witch, Madge is also a fortune-teller, and when the bridesmaids surround her, although they don't actually believe she can see into the future, they want to know what the future is. Effie, being the bride, steps forward first. She's unafraid of what the witch might say because she's young enough to believe that nothing bad will ever happen. Holding out the palm of her hand she's almost challenging Madge, and Madge accepts her challenge. Some versions of the story have her shuffling a deck of cards, looking into the cards and then out at the bridesmaids, predicting that some will bear healthy children while others will not. Then, for Effie, she takes a crystal ball from a black sack at her feet. She's like the carnival character in *The Wizard of Oz* who later plays the part of the Wizard. It's the scene in which Dorothy, having run away from home, finds herself in his sideshow trailer getting her fortune read. The carnival man, peering into his crystal ball, tells her to close her eyes, and finding in her basket the photo of a woman, he tells her that someone loves her, and she says, Auntie Em. And he says yes, her name is Emily, and although he can't actually see her future he can see that the girl loves someone, and is loved. And you can see in him the soothsayer's sadness, knowing her future is probably sadness, certainly death, and the power of prophecy has probably made Madge a little bitter. She tells Effie that she will have many children. And will they be happy? Yes. And my marriage, that will be happy? Yes. And this gives Effie the confidence to ask if James loves her more than anything else in the world. When she asks the question she looks over at James, sitting on a straight-backed chair, feet planted, hands on knees, knees pointing forward ahead, trying to smile. Effie is looking at James when Madge tells her no, that her future lies with someone else. Pause. But you said I'd be happily married. And Madge tells her she *will* be happily married. To Gurn. Which is ridiculous. Everyone knows it's ridiculous. James does too, and the rage that's sparked in him, starting in his stomach, or just below, works its way up into his chest where it pushes against his ribs and his neck and it's like a trigger, the feeling, and fueled by that feeling he attacks the old witch, and not just verbally. He knows he's getting carried away but he's carried away, carried by something, and standing in front of Madge, close enough to be threatening, when she responds by being *un*threatened, he uses his arms to herd her, like a beast, and that's what she is, and beasts should be kept outside, and he never hits her but when he pushes her out the door there's a violence that Effie, oddly, finds reassuring. She's not mad. She believes his anger is an expression of his love, and that's all she wants, to feel his love, and he really does care for her, and when he looks into her eyes he forgets, at least momentarily, about his visions.

It was raining the night Cornell went to see Tamara dance Giselle. Like *La Sylphide*, *Giselle* is about impossible love, and although he sat in the balcony, because he'd brought binoculars he could see her body when she danced, her arms stretching out and her toes barely touching the stage. But mainly he watched her face. She was an actor as well as a dancer, and he could see the joy on her face when, as Giselle, she fell in love. After the performance the usherette must have been puzzled by this odd old man with a brown package knocking on the door of the prima ballerina. And Tamara was there, still in costume, her face still glowing with the glow of a sixteen- or fifteen- or seventeen-year-old girl. She was happy to receive him and receive the gift he'd brought. She asked him to sit, untied the brown paper wrapping and what he'd brought was a box, small, velvet lined, with objects from his collection, a piece of crystal, a drawing of a bird in flight, a photograph of a ballerina dressed as a black swan. She liked it, he could tell, and she set it beside her dressing-table mirror. She was in front of the mirror, loosening her hair and removing her makeup, and Cornell wasn't much of a talker but she didn't mind. She told him about the performance, about her fouettés and the mistakes she'd made, and when she talked about her mother's annoying habits, he mentioned his own mother's way of intruding on *his* life. While they were talking she stepped behind a folding screen near the door, and as she talked she removed her costume. He stood up to go. He didn't want to intrude. But no, she said, stay, and when she said it she was standing so that he could see her face, held aloft, or it seemed to him aloft, and her long neck and her bare shoulders, and I think if there was a moment, that was the moment he fell in love with her. Stay, she said, and he wanted to make her happy so he did. Like a lover, he adored her, and like a lover he wanted to know her, and in his imagination he did. In his mind she was his lover, and like his lover, like any lovers in a Romantic ballet, their love was doomed. *La Sylphide. Giselle. Swan Lake*, *La Bayadère*. It was always the same. The lovers could never be together because fate had made it impossible, and it *was* impossible, he knew that. She was spirit, pure and ethereal, and there he was, sitting in the straight-backed chair, feet planted, thin and quiet, and he doesn't even know how to dance.

When it comes to expressing human emotion, the flowing lines of a dancer's body are perfect for joy. Also hope and longing. Anger on the other hand, and more complicated emotions like disappointment and regret, they're expressed in ballet with pantomime. When Effie and her fellow ballerinas skip off to prepare for the wedding celebration, James, left alone, can't really dance what he feels, this knot in his chest. He's thinking about Effie and thinking about the Sylph, and he would like to believe that he doesn't need to choose between them. But he does. He knows he can't have both, and that's why he's making a fist. He's battling within himself, thinking of a path his life could take and fighting the urge to take it. But the urge is there, and whether his imagination calls her into being, or whether it's just a coincidence, the Sylph appears in the room. Like stepping out of a mist, she glides up to him, and when she points to the tears in her eyes he can see her sadness and he can feel the love he has. For her. And her? She's sad because their love is impossible. He loves someone else, someone human, and she would like to be human, to experience human emotions, and she's excited by the idea of love, but her heart is also afraid, thinking of how that idea might realize itself. What would the mechanics of that realization be? She doesn't know because she's innocent. But she's also brave, and she allows herself to confess her love to him, a confession that sounds like truth, and the verbalization of that truth emboldens her. She becomes flirtatious, pulling off his tartan scarf and wrapping it around her delicate neck and delicate shoulders, standing on the very points of her toes, which is amazing to him and he can't resist. She isn't just beautiful. She's beauty itself, and captivated by that beauty he reaches out to hold her, and once he has her in his arms, he kisses her, and there's no question anymore if she's real because he knows she's real because he can taste her. And she tastes him. They don't even know they're dancing, intoxicated by the warm metallic taste that seals them together, and they don't notice Gurn, watching from behind the stairs. They don't notice him running up the stairs to the room where Effie and her bridesmaids are putting on their wedding clothes. Gurn knocks on the door but he doesn't wait. He barges in. The girls cover themselves but Gurn is looking at the floor, doing his duty. He believes he's just stating the facts as he saw them, unaware of the pleasure he feels when he makes his report about James and the girl. What girl? She had wings, he says. Wings? I think she had wings. And of course they don't believe him. Effie is aware that Gurn has a

crush on her, even loves her, and that awareness makes him unbelievable. But he's insistent, like a salesman, so she agrees to
walk down the steep wooden stairs and check for herself. And
at different moments in the ballet I identify with different characters, and I'm oddly sympathetic now to what Gurn must be
feeling, about his friend, a friend he thought he knew, and did
know, and respected, but now it's his turn. And James, having
heard the footsteps on the stairs, has instructed the Sylph to hide
in the armchair, under a red plaid blanket. When no mysterious
female being is visible in the room, Gurn accuses James of hiding her. He looks behind curtains and behind doors, and there's
someone here, a girl. But there's no one. But Gurn knows there
is someone because he saw someone, and he knows it's a trick
and James is worried. There's the chair, and beneath the blanket
there's a large lump and Gurn challenges his friend. What's beneath the blanket? James is about to be found out, and he knows
that denial will make it worse but what can he do. There's no one
here, he says. So let's just take a look, Gurn says, and he goes to
the blanket, takes hold of the material and lifts it up to reveal
to the world the truth that will change his life but there's nothing there. Like the sitcom I used to watch, *My Favorite Martian*.
A Martian is stranded on Earth, trying to get home, not revealing what he is because of bigotry and prejudice, and a young
man has taken him in but the landlady is suspicious. And it's always at the moment when she's just about to reveal him to the
world that something happens. And now the chair is empty. The
guests assume Gurn made the story up, out of jealousy, and they
tease him, and the teasing, which is playful, leads to dancing.
Gurn sulks off to a corner, and although James takes the hand
of his intended, his partnering is halfhearted. The Sylph is still

in the room. He sees her shadow on the floor, or thinks he does, and in a video of Rudolph Nureyev playing the part, when he catches sight of the girl dancing with the other ballerinas, invisible to them but dancing their steps, swirling under their outstretched arms, his face lights up. You can see his expression and gesture and the dancing itself is excited by emotion. And he's improvising. He's finding his way. And I've tried to do that, to live fully in that moment when love appears, and allow it to appear, but it's hard. It means not surrendering to the hopelessness of what will eventually happen. And during the divertissement, when partners are exchanged, as James tries to position himself to be with the object of his desire, he discovers the confusion of not knowing. Is he dancing with the Sylph or with Effie? Every time he thinks it might be her it's always Effie, and when the dance ends and the Sylph disappears he finds himself holding Effie by the waist. She turns, looks up, and seeing Effie's eyes, which are loving eyes, although it's not as exciting as looking into the eyes of a dream, he finds relief, you can feel it, at being with an actual person.

Just as you can only love a limited number of people, there are only a limited number of people you can be in a lifetime. I was still in my twenties then, newly arrived in Los Angeles, not a writer or an artist or anything really, just knowing that what I was had come to nothing, that I *had* nothing, and unable to live with that I started spending time with Cosmo. I was looking for possible role models, and Cosmo was someone I was attracted to, someone you might have called charismatic, and part of his charisma was his ability, or his need really, to make the world seem like a party. And he always seemed to have the invitation.

So I went along with him, and I watched him, and although it's impossible to be someone else, by imitating a person you can get the characteristics of that person to adhere to you, or in my case, adhere to me, not that I imitated everything Cosmo did. Some of what he did didn't interest me. The limousine, for instance. Hiring a limousine wasn't embarrassing for Cosmo because he made riding in a limousine, and drinking champagne in the back of a limousine, part of who he was. And there I was, with him, sitting beside a sealed window, Cosmo at the other window, and Rachel was sitting between us. She was a dancer, tall, dark skinned, and Cosmo, having offered her a job at his club, was showing her the town. He was wooing her, wearing his regular evening costume, a rumpled tuxedo. I had on a sport coat he'd given me and Rachel, shoulder to shoulder with us, had a purple orchid pinned to her chest, a small black purse in her lap, and like a deer she was beautiful, keen and alert, or maybe Cosmo and I were the deer and she was the headlight, her earrings catching the light from the streetlights as we drove. And because Cosmo was trying to make her happy, and because he associated drinking with happiness, he pulled a bottle of champagne from the backseat ice bucket. He handed me a glass, and Rachel wasn't drinking, and I told him I was fine but he reached out to me with the champagne bottle, reaching over Rachel's body, and I suppose his idea was to make me happier than I was, but I was happy enough. And Cosmo was handsome, not perfect, with his large nose, more strong than large, and his sly smile, like a fox smiling, although I've never seen a fox smile, and his eyes. I have seen stars twinkling, and he had a cigarette in one hand, and although he was the owner of a nightclub, he always seemed like a salesman. He had what salesmen have, persistence, and he was trying to find the mouth of my champagne flute with the mouth of the champagne bottle, but I can be persistent too. And I was, except after a while he wore you down. They call it the force of personality but really it's just wearing you down, and I didn't want to drink champagne but he wouldn't take no for an answer. So I let him fill my flute, the bubbles rising up from inside the liquid, rising up and breaking the surface, and I'm sure Cosmo ordered the finest, so I drank. Which made Cosmo happy, which made me happy. And the smile he smiled at Rachel triggered in her, and to some extent it triggered in me, not triggered but when Cosmo laughed, although I didn't know what was supposed to be funny, and although whatever it was had already turned into something else, we felt it, the carelessness of happiness, and we were all in a jovial mood when we arrived at the Ship Ahoy.

In *La Sylphide*, the wedding ceremony takes place near a church, on a grassy rise overlooking the river. Chairs have been brought for the older people, and standing behind the chairs are the friends, mainly Effie's friends, all Effie's friends in fact. James has no friends. Except Gurn, who's in an odd position. He wants to wish his old friend well but his jealousy is making that difficult. He's looking around, hoping the Sylph will appear but when she does appear, because she's a sylph, she's invisible to him and to everyone but James. People notice the wind in the trees or the leaves falling, but James can see her behind the leaves, gliding from one tree to another, inviting him to come closer. He's standing by the altar now, watching her while everyone has turned to watch the bride, beautiful and white, and the Sylph is asking James to love her, and to prove his love by dancing with her. And when Effie stands beside James, her husband-to-be, she's not aware of his distraction because she's distracted by her own emotions. And as the priest reads the text and as the couple are about to solemnly swear their vows, and their lives, and exchange their rings, the Sylph appears behind the priest. James is about to do as he's instructed, to place his ring on Effie's finger, and that's when the unseen Sylph reaches out from behind the robes of the priest, snatches the ring, and slides it over her finger. And because she's invisible it looks like the ring is rising of its own accord, sliding onto what looks like thin air but it's her. And she's not invisible to James. He can see her and hear her and he understands what she's telling him, that she'll die without him. Then she runs down the hill and into the forest by the river. The priest is bewildered. The guests are bewildered. No one can tell exactly what happened because no one could see the invisible hand. And they're even more bewildered when James suddenly takes off running, running *after* something, or *away* from something, they don't know because they don't see the girl. And the Sylph is not dumb. She knows when she dashes off into the forest she's enticing James, and the root of *entice* is *to set on fire*, and James can feel the fire inside his body, and without thinking he makes the decision to chase what fuels that fire. His idea is to save the girl by loving her, and Gurn, who loves Effie, probably feels good. He's been vindicated. You see, I was right about the girl, and I was right about James. But Effie can't listen. James is running away from me, that's what she thinks, and the root of *distraught* is *to tear apart*, and she tears herself away, running back into the church, followed by James's mother, who tries to console her, and Gurn is also there, his hand on her back, patting her back but she's inconsolable. And that's when Madge appears. Really she'd been there the whole time, but when the lights change, there she is, sitting in a pew, and Effie is next to her, in front of the altar, her face buried in the seat of the pew and Madge, when she tells Effie she has to forget about James, takes the girl's head in her hand and turns the head, directing its gaze at Gurn.

The Bakery Girl of Monceau is the first of what Eric Rohmer called his Moral Tales. It's a short film, twenty minutes long, but in it a lifetime of choice is condensed into a ménage à trois that takes place in the narrator's mind. A young man, walking down the street with a pal, sees a beautiful young girl who he talks to, and she talks to him, and they arrange to meet. And the young man is elated until he realizes, when he tries to find her, that he's lost her address. In Rohmer there's often someone getting the wrong address, and so the next day the narrator rings what he thinks is her bell, and when there's no answer he wanders around her neighborhood. Day after day he does this, until he's almost but not quite ready to give up. He stops at a bakery to have a pastry. He talks to the bakery girl. He enjoys the pastry, and he enjoys the flirtation with the girl, and he's the one who initiates it. Although the bakery girl is not as beautiful as the first girl, she's young and therefore eager, and they enjoy each other's attention. He enjoys the role of the older man, and he makes it a habit, to stop every day and have a pastry, gradually forgetting about the first girl because his flirting with the bakery girl becomes more than flirting. He begins wooing her. And she likes being wooed, and because the movie is told from his point of view we can't know for sure but it seems as if she's falling in love with him. It's obvious she likes him. And by this point he's stopped thinking about the first girl, following the trajectory of the story, getting more and more intimate with the bakery girl until finally he asks her for a date. The girl is cautious, she wants him to promise he's not just leading her on, and no, he assures her, and they find a time that's suitable for both of them, and on the appointed day, on his way to the bakery, he runs into the first girl. She's walking on crutches. Apparently she broke her ankle, which is why she wasn't able to answer her door but now she's feeling better. And the heart of the movie is his decision. To honor his date with the bakery girl or to forget his promise and be with the woman who now seems to be the one he might actually love. In the movie it's not clear what he'll do but of course he leaves the bakery girl waiting for him, walks off with the beautiful girl and basically that's the story. Rohmer said the movie's subtitle, *A Moral Tale*, didn't refer to what was moral in the sense of being decent and honorable, but rather to the fact that all our relationships with people have moral implications, filled with decisions about how we choose to be.

Unlike Cosmo's club, the Ship Ahoy was a club for gambling. The men who ran it weren't mobsters exactly, or gangsters, but when we stepped out of the limousine, still holding our champagne flutes, someone must have recognized Cosmo because a door opened and a large man, like a bodyguard, led us down a hallway and into a low room with a sprayed acoustic ceiling. A picture window framed a view of the dark harbor, and there was a round table in the middle of the room, with chairs, and a few men were sitting in the chairs. That was the poker game. Rachel and I were given seats along the wall, our backs against its faux wood paneling, and I watched Cosmo walk to the table like walking into another room, a brightly lit room that put everything else in darkness, including me. And Rachel. Which doesn't mean we weren't taken care of. Waiters brought us pastries and dipping sauce, and yes, I was drinking. First of all, the drinks were free, and once you cross the line of drinking, it's hard to draw the line because the line is already behind you. And although I'd told myself I wouldn't drink too much, I wasn't listening to myself. Plus, I was sitting next to Rachel. I was sitting on a gold, slightly padded convention-hall chair, and the place had a nautical theme. Fishing nets and life preservers, and anchors were hung along the walls. The waiters were serving us seafood wrapped in bacon. I assumed that Rachel and I, since there was nothing else to do, would talk, but the way the chairs were set against the wall, it was like we were an audience, or at a trial, facing the round table in the center of the room, and I've never been to the Colosseum in Rome but it must have been like this, with the poker table where the gladiators would have battled. And because the table was our focal point, although we couldn't see the details of the game, we were both looking in the direction of the five men, watching them holding cards, pushing chips to the center of the table. The room was cool and the chair I was sitting on was cool, and I was wishing I had something engaging to say. I knew the harder I tried to be engaging, the less engaging I would be, so I asked her a simple question about her job at Cosmo's club. And we talked a little, about performing and nakedness, and it was a nice enough conversation but when it was over, when she turned her attention back to the poker game, that's when I noticed the goose bumps on my arm. Or goose flesh. It appears when the tiny muscles attached to the base of our hair follicles contract, something to do with the fight-or-flight response, or sexual arousal, and I mention it because Rachel was sitting very straight, her neck long, her arm bones pulled into their sockets, and because she was staring off toward the poker game she didn't know I was following her follicles, from her wrist to her arm, the fine hairs tracing a path up her neck, over her ear and I noticed a mole near her hairline. I didn't want to stare but I felt myself getting lost, in her, and in the thoughts that arise when you're absorbed by your own concentration on something, and I was surprised when a man, a large man, stepped up to us, me specifically, and in a hollow voice said something about offering me a seat. At the table. I wasn't sure what he was talking about. The card-playing table? Apparently one of the players had left and now a seat had opened up, and this could be one of those moments, I thought, when you can change the course of your life. The man's name was Freddie, and I could see Cosmo waving me over, but I don't even play poker. I play, but I've never been very good, never really enjoyed it, although my father was excellent poker player. He used to play with Gregory Peck, the movie star. He called him Eldred Peck, said Eldred still owed him twenty dollars, and from him I learned the basic elements of poker, the most interesting being the bluff. Since no one knows what cards are held by the other players, if you can make a player think you have a winning hand, it's possible to win with a terrible hand. Which requires acting. Which requires psychology. Which is interesting to me because I like to watch the way people walk, the muscles they use, but I don't consider myself an actor. But Rachel was telling me to join the game, to go play, to have some fun, and Cosmo was signaling me, so I stood up and followed the signal. I followed this Freddie person, who said that any friend of Cosmo's, and he didn't say what about any friend of Cosmo's, but it felt good to be

respected, or a friend of someone respected, and with his mas-
sive hand spread across my latissimus he guided me to the table
where he pulled out the chair that had been occupied by someone and now was occupied by me. And the chair was probably
radiating heat but I didn't notice because I was feeling the excitement of joining the game. Whatever chemical causes elation, I was feeling a surge of it, looking around at the men at the
table, all of them older than I was, most of them smoking cigars,
drinking amber-colored drinks which turned out to be whiskey,
and I'll have one too. If I was going to cross the line, I might as
well dive in. A waiter brought me a glass of scotch with one rock,
a single piece of ice melting in the alcohol. Introductions were
made, people nodded, and the dealer asked me how many chips
I would like, meaning how many chips did I want to buy. Ah-
hah, I thought. We were going to be using real money. I didn't
think of that when I let myself get led to the table.

The story begins with *La Sylphide* because, apart from being the
first Romantic ballet, it has an interesting witch. The music isn't
as good as Tchaikovsky's but when the second act begins, when
the curtain rises, we see Madge, not dancing because witches
don't quite dance in Romantic ballet but if they did it would look
like this. A clearing in the forest. Madge and her two compan-
ions, also witches, are swaying and writhing, waving their arms
around a boiling cauldron, calling for revenge. They're not actually saying the word *revenge* because their sense of grievance has
made the object of their revenge unimportant. The whole world,
they seem to say, will do just nicely. And I say *cauldron* but it's just
a large pot, like the boiling vat in Shakespeare's Scottish play except the ballet witches dancing around this pot are a little more

sexual. That's how it looks to me. Their anger is erotic, or they've made it erotic, and according to what I've read, in modern versions of the ballet the witches perform a striptease. They unbutton their dark cloaks, letting them fall off their strong shoulders, and by revealing what they are they're challenging the world to accept what they are, underneath. And I say *underneath* because from the earth they draw their power. They're creatures of the natural world, using their knowledge of the natural world to make what seems like magic to us because the natural world is mysterious to us. They call on the earth and the trees and the sky, and what they're trying to do is alter the course of events. And you do that by making choices. You move to a new city, make friends with a stranger. Events in your life are altered by the choices you make and the witches take that one step further. They're altering the choices *other* people make. Madge instructs her sister witches, telling them what herbs and tinctures go into the pot, and nakedness at this point isn't gratuitous because it connects the contradictions of what they're doing, the science of what they're doing with the magic. Unlike Taglioni dancing the Sylph, the witches dance in a style called terre à terre, their feet never leaving the ground. Their hands move in circles above the pot, their guttural recitation blending into the ingredients of the pot, and what makes this scene notable is the fact that the witches, being played by men, allow themselves to be men. Men playing women. Therefore both man and woman. Androgyny gives them power, and when the spell has been finally cast, and Madge pulls a scarf from the steaming liquid, the scarf has been transformed.

I knew enough about poker to know that a large percentage of winning is luck. And although I'd never won a lottery, or won anything really, I'd always thought of myself as having an amicable relationship with fortune. You can't will luck or create it, all you can do is allow a space where it feels welcome and comfortable, and that's what I was doing. Cosmo was across the table, to my right, and at the beginning I imitated his style, the way he fingered his pile of chips. By imitating his style I got not only a feel for the game but also a confidence in my ability to play. When the dealer dealt our cards, some faceup, some facedown, I was being a beginner. And I had what they call beginner's luck. Although I didn't win the first hand I did win the second, and the bets weren't big because they didn't want to scare me away, and as the game went on my imitation of Cosmo was doing better than the actual Cosmo. I knew to quit when I was ahead, to wait for the wave and then ride the wave. And I knew when a bald man with a mustache was bluffing me, trying to make me think he had a better hand than he did. I had three nines, which wasn't fantastic but I had a hunch, and a hunch is an intimation of luck, invisible but swirling around us and in us, and I kept up with the man, betting as much as he did, and in fact betting most of my money, and it wasn't confidence but was just as good, and when we finally presented our cards my three nines beat his three sevens. I couldn't tell if Rachel, sitting against the wall, was watching me but if she was she would have seen that my pile of chips was growing. The chips were different colors, in denominations of five, ten, twenty, fifty, and one hundred dollars, and I was up quite a few hundred dollars. I didn't count my chips, why tempt superstition, and the night went on like that, me winning occasionally, and yes, I was losing too, you can't help but lose a little, but I was getting used to losing and winning, and also I was drinking. I changed my order from scotch on ice to gin and tonic, heavy on the tonic I told the waiter, and I knew that drinking too much wasn't good, that being inebriated wouldn't assist me in my quest, which was less about winning and more about being a person who could wait for the waves of luck and then ride them. I would have been content to break even, to enjoy the play of the game, and in fact as I sipped the gin and tonics, and as the game continued, I lost enough of my chips to put me back where I came from, financially. I still felt that luck, like a friend or a lover or a sense of self, was hovering nearby. Like a seed, blown on the wind, and once it falls to earth it needs the right kind of soil, the right amount of water and sunlight, and although there's no guarantee, I was pretty sure luck would eventually pop up, like a tree, or a plant, and until it did I kept playing. Playing and drinking, and I wasn't drunk but I wasn't myself, that's the expression, *not quite myself,* and it's natural to lose a little. Cosmo was also losing. And I wasn't losing a lot. But enough. Not desperate yet, but I didn't want to miss the moment when luck would eventually return. So I kept making bets, and because I was aware they were unintelligent bets I felt I was in control of my losing, and by remaining in control, when the time came, I would also control my rise back up to the break-even point. The question was, when would that time come. Everyone at the table was waiting for that time. Cosmo, my normally effusive friend, was quiet, relaxed, not looking up at me, or when he did, not expressing any concern or encouragement, and although his self-sufficient relaxation was worthy of emulation, when I tried to sit like he sat, elbows down, cards held at my heart, I didn't feel what sitting like him felt like.

James at this point is totally in love. He's wandering the forest looking for his vision. She's a vision but she's real, and he's

walking down a muddy logging road into a stand of old-growth
oaks and then something happens I don't quite understand. He
finds a bird's nest on the ground, with an egg inside. He carries it
with him as he walks, walking along until at some point the Sylph
appears, floating by his side. It's you, he says, and she smiles, but
when he reaches out she jumps back, out of his reach. It's playful in a way, and when the ballet was staged in Paris they had
wires attached to the ballerina and like magic, when she jumped
she actually left the ground, hovering. And James, as a way to
get her back to earth, offers her the bird's nest as a gift. And the
part I don't understand is her reaction. When she sees the egg
inside the nest she pantomimes fear, telling him with her hands,
get that thing away from me. Is she afraid the egg might take
his affection? Or is she sad, like Taglioni, thinking of the egg
separated from its mother, as Taglioni must have been separated,
spending every day with a father who forced her to practice, and
I used to watch my own daughter in her ballet class, her little
pink leotard, and even the beginner's class is fraught with failure,
and once a week is not so bad but every day, and with her own
father, or maybe that's what she wanted. Or does the egg repre-
sent procreation? The Sylph is partly human but she's unable to
have children, and maybe the egg reminds her of what she cannot have, and she must know that James is also something she
cannot have but she can't help it. She wants it, and the desire she
has takes up so much room in her mind that it's all she knows.
She doesn't say anything, but she lowers herself, or she gets low-
ered, and when she lands next to James, covered by the thin fabric of her dress, a tutu, a long tutu, she beckons him. She beckons
him forward but when he takes a step forward she jumps away.
His arms are still outspread, an invitation to hug, just a friendly

hug, but she's not allowing herself to be touched. And he won-
ders if he made a mistake, if she actually is an illusion, because if
she isn't an illusion, why would she be so difficult? She dances a
solo for him, and a little dancing is fine, and yes, she performs
her solo with brilliance, and people talk about line in ballet,
meaning an imaginary line running from the tip of the ballerina's toe, spiraling up her body, lifting her neck and head, and
even in an arabesque, with her legs and her arms all stretched
in separate directions, an inner perfection was revealed in her
form. And James is entranced by that inner beauty, radiating outward, and that's why he wants to hold her. He wants to kiss her
again and feel her body next to his, and there's no one around, no
need for hiding their love but that's what she does when she summons her fellow sylphs, all dressed in white, all young and fresh
faced. They dance to entertain him, but also to distract him from
the fact that the Sylph is unattainable. Longing for her is all you
can have, and Cosmo dated a transvestite once. She also wouldn't
allow herself to be touched. Which drove him crazy. And James,
knowing why the Sylph is afraid, tells her the difference between
them, the fact that they're two different species, doesn't matter.
He wants her. He declares his love for her. And she's thrilled.
And he's thrilled that she's thrilled because now his dream will
finally come true, she'll finally solidify and embrace him, and
that's when she and her fellow sylphs fly off.

Erik Bruhn, who danced in *La Sylphide*, said of James: *Nothing
can actually get hold of him; not his mother, his fiancée, none of the
real people understand him. But when he is alone with his dream
he is quite himself.* And he's alone now, deep in the shadows of the
forest when Madge appears. She steps out of a shadow and she's

friendly enough. Apparently she's forgotten how he treated her, or she's risen above it, and because he's so wrapped up in his desire to unite with the Sylph he forgets he doesn't like her. He tells her his problem, the problem of longing, and she feigns her good intentions. She talks compassionately and sympathetically, and by way of ending his dilemma she pulls out the magic scarf. With this, she says, you can capture her, and keep her, and she demonstrates how to use it by covering James where his wings would be. She describes the rapturous effect the scarf will have, and when she places the scarf in his hands she tells him to practice on her, and when he drapes the material over her bony scapula, palpable under the sackcloth, she turns to him, her mouth open, her tongue crouched inside, and this is when he remembers she's a witch. She's bringing her lips closer to his and, wait a minute, he says, but she's holding the hair at the back of his skull, and she's a man, so she's strong, pulling him closer, telling him how, if he covers his lover's wings with the scarf, the wings will fall off, and she tells him to kiss her lips.

Even in the middle of Manhattan, walking down the crowded streets, Joseph Cornell was alone with his dream. And often the dream was a girl. He watched the girls he had crushes on, the girls he saw on the streets, salesgirls and coworkers, and one of these girls he met while he was punching his time card at work. He saw a quality in her that transcended her surroundings, a grace that induced him to start following her, like a spy, never getting close to her and rarely speaking with her but building up an imaginary world she inhabited. Many of these girls were given drawings or boxes, but his relationship with Tamara Toumanova, who had danced for Diaghilev, was different. Sharing secrets about their lives gave them a connection he'd never had before, and during one of their conversations, after or before a ballet, he invited her to visit his studio in Queens. And the day she arrived, before she arrived, he was agitated, nervous and worried that his meddlesome mother might say something or do something to embarrass him. Tamara and his mother lived in separate worlds, but when Tamara arrived his mother was charmed. As was his brother. But Tamara was his, and he shooed his mother up the stairs so he could be alone with her, the two of them drinking tea at the kitchen table. He watched her arms. She'd taken off her coat and was talking about Russian tea and Russian dolls, and he was watching the fabric of her dress, and the folds of the fabric, watching her loose hair falling across her ears and down her long, delicate neck. Then he showed Tamara his workshop. They walked down the steep steps and he offered her a chair and he sat at his table and he wanted to see more of her. Not see her *again*, although he would like to do that, and he didn't say more of her skin and flesh but he wanted more than a button or piece of earring. She was wearing woolen slacks, and it was warm down there and he asked her if she would be willing to pose for him. Certainly, she said, and she slipped off her shoe, set her foot on the seat of the chair and leaned back, striking a pose, her hands extending from her arms. He opened a sketch-book, but because he wasn't a very good draftsman it took him a while to start drawing. It was a portrait of her, and he kept looking at her, not drawing but staring at her face and her collar-bones, and how would you like me to be, she said, and her face was too perfect and she was too perfect and he looked at her face and loved her face, but he wanted more than her face. She was young and strong, and he was already an old man by then, old but in love with her, and he asked her if she would pose in the nude. She declined, politely, and he went on drawing, and when he finished the portrait he gave it to her but it was awkward, even he could sense that. On his next visit to her dressing room he saw the portrait, propped against her dressing room mirror. He was watching her from his usual chair, and when he presented her with another box she thanked him, as she always did, and she gave him in return an object for his collection, a green glass button from one of her costumes. She set the box with the other boxes he'd made for her, and she liked the boxes but she liked other things too. And other people. Joseph Cornell wasn't the only one who wanted to keep her company. She was a famous ballerina, and ballet was big back then, and because of her fame, and because her dancing was known by people who wanted to be near that fame, other people were knocking on her door. She was receiving visitors, men wearing fur, and women too, but mainly men, and she invited them in. Before it had been just the two of them, but now her room was crowded with people, other people, and Cornell sat in his chair and these other people, with their importance or self-importance, represented a world that didn't include him. They stood, surrounding Tamara, and she was the sun and they were the planets, and if the scene was from a Romantic ballet then he wasn't the hero, the James or the Prince or the Nureyev. He was the sylph who could never be loved. He was the creature that didn't fit, and these men and women were part of a life he wasn't part of, and would never be part of, and he didn't want to be part of it but there he was, sitting in the corner and no one even noticed him. And at first he told himself he didn't mind, but gradually he began to realize what it meant, and what he meant to her, and he realized their dressing room conversations had come to an end. She kissed his cheeks when he left, but she was kissing a lot of cheeks, and when he walked out of the dressing room, into the night, the love he'd felt for her, and the desire he'd felt to be near her, watching her and studying her, had already begun to fade.

The way hunters walk through a forest, in parallel lines, beating the undergrowth to flush out their prey, that's how the wedding guests are searching for James. And when Gurn finds a hat by a tree he thinks that James has been taken, or he's gone, dead preferably, and when Madge appears behind him he asks her if in fact he *is* dead. She tells him to propose to Effie. But is he dead? Ask her now, she says, but Gurn believes that Effie can never be his, that she's too beautiful. But the story of *La Sylphide* is full of self-deception. James, for his part, wants to believe his desire, because it's forbidden, is unconscious, and because it's unconscious it's more powerful than he is. And the Sylph wants to believe the same thing, that by avoiding desire she's fueling desire, including her own. And Gurn also wants to believe that he might be someone that Effie could love. But because Effie loves someone else he needs a spell. And Old Madge gives him one, a pill that she carefully places in the center of his palm. In some versions he kneels, and she places the pill under his tongue, and when he finally gets back to the lodge he finds Effie playing pool with her friends. They're pretending to play but really they're too sad. Effie's swollen face is evidence that she's been crying, and when Gurn speaks to her he doesn't mention the hat he found. And he doesn't know if the pill is doing it, or if *he's* doing it, but he finds himself feeling the courage or confidence or whatever it is that allows him to say what another self would say, what he would say but has never been able to, and now he takes Effie's hand. He takes the pool cue out of her hand, and it's probably the pill because his genitals feel tingly. He's surrounded by all her friends but he doesn't notice them, it's just the two of them, and when he asks her to marry him Effie, recalling the prophecy of the old witch, although this isn't what she wanted to happen, accepts.

The way to change an undesirable situation is to change the situation's direction, and the secret of changing direction is to start early, preferably at the beginning, or if the beginning isn't possible just start again. I guessed it had something to do with breathing. So I took a breath. Out with the old, in with the new. Out with my bad luck and in with the thick smoke of cigarettes. The air-conditioning was rumbling on a nearby wall but the room was still smoky. Rachel was still in her chair, still young, and the men at the table were mostly heavy, some with gray hair, three or four of them very tan. They kept their heads down, even Cosmo, so as not to accidentally reveal in their faces the contents of their cards. I was watching them and Rachel was too, and watching me, and although I wasn't playing against Cosmo, and although she was going to work for Cosmo, I imagined she might be rooting for me. *Lady Luck* is a term from the movies, the Westerns, and we weren't in a saloon but I felt her watching me as I sipped my drink and I laughed occasionally when a joke was told. The voices of the men when they spoke were deep, their hands thick, and they would have been intimidating in my normal life but now I wasn't in my normal life. I was drunk first of all, and I was losing money, and I should have ordered a sandwich, that might have helped, but the cards kept coming, and it was exhausting, the concentration involved in hoping the cards would be the cards I wanted, the cards that would help me win, but I wasn't winning. In fact I was losing so much that at one point, the dealer, a bald man with a double chin, asked me if I needed a loan. He called it a marker. A few thousand dollars. A man called Seymour appeared from behind a glass door. He had a bushy mustache and he glanced at me when he told the dealer to let me keep playing. And a few thousand dollars wasn't so much, and Cosmo was doing it too, borrowing from something that seemed like a bank, and I played with the money until, when my chips ran out, I needed a new marker. I assured the dealer my credit was good. Cosmo can vouch for me, that's what I said, and when Seymour appeared again, looking at me, although Cosmo didn't speak up, my loan was approved. And with this money I would have to be careful. But not too careful because being too careful gets you nowhere. But careful enough. And I was. At a certain point I felt my luck returning, and thank god because playing and losing is not as much fun as playing and winning, and I started winning again, and betting more, and the game is simple. Know when to hold 'em, know when to fold 'em, and I was almost back to even when I made the mistake, or the miscalculation, of assuming that the cards in my hand were better than the cards of the man I was playing against. He never addressed me, which I didn't like, and his carefully combed hair was too carefully combed. And maybe I let my dislike influence my decision to stay in the game, to borrow more money. My luck would return, that's how it goes, not in circles exactly but it flits from one flower to the next, like a bee, and we were the flowers and I was due for a visitation. I definitely felt that my time was coming, and when the loan was approved I felt certain it was here, the confluence of money and luck, and I attempted a bluff, holding nothing but a pair of sixes, and because it's psychology I acted, or tried to act, as if I was trying to act as if I had a terrible hand because I wanted the men at the table to think that I was trying to act like I had a good hand because I had a bad hand when really I did have a good hand, and it was confusing, even to me, the levels of subterfuge. Long story short, I lost. But because I'd gotten so close I was pretty sure luck was close. The next round was dealt, and I wasn't praying because I wouldn't know how to begin, something like, oh god, please let me have a good hand, or please smile on me, or please, if you give me this then I'll do whatever you want, something like that. More effective would have been to relax, take a breath, look at my cards and remember the fun I'd had at the beginning of the game. That would have been good but I'd lost too much money now, and it wasn't even *my* money. And why was I here, drinking these drinks? I asked the waiters to make them weak but I was feeling them, and I wanted to stop but I had to keep going, claw myself back, pull myself by my bootstraps, whatever that means. And I tried to be cunning, like a suitor, pretending I didn't care about luck, letting luck take an interest in me if it wanted to, and if it wanted to it could sit on my lap. And when the cards were dealt mine were good, better than good, and bets were placed and I needed another loan if I was to stay in the game, and that's when Seymour walked in, the glass doors closing behind him. He seemed to know exactly what was happening and he told the dealer my credit was cut off. Cut off? That's impossible. I need to win my money back. I told Seymour, who was walking away, that I could pay them back, but how could I pay them back. I looked at Cosmo, his tapered fingers stroking his cards, and although he was also losing he had a smile, the faintest stretch of a smile across his lips and sure, he had collateral, I had nothing. I had no house, and my car was falling apart, and then the man named Freddie was standing behind me, pulling out my chair, helping me to stand, and when I did stand, that was the end of the game for me.

La Sylphide is based, in part, on an opera, which was based on a legend, which is based on a person named Robert the Devil. In the story a young woman, unable to conceive a child, after nights of prayer, goes to the devil, asks for help, and he obliges her by giving her a son. And being the devil's son he's prone to acts of terror, to remorseless havoc and raping and murder and one day it dawns on him what he is, that he is bad, and he wants to change what he is. People tell him it's impossible to change but something has to change and so he visits his mother and learns from her that he's made of the devil. Instead of bemoaning his fate or cursing heaven, he works to banish the devilish part of who he is, cleansing himself of the evil in him. In the course of the opera he learns to subdue himself, to *thwart the designs of that accursed fiend* who created him, who has made of him an instrument of destruction and of sin, and in the end he becomes righteous. His goodness is rewarded. He's offered a beautiful woman to be his wife, and although in some versions of the story he marries her, in most versions he becomes a hermit living in the wilderness.

James is sitting on the gnarled root of an old tree, leaning against the tree's trunk, his knees near his chest, looking at the dead leaves at his feet. Often he holds his head in his hands in a gesture of dejection. He's told himself, and now he realizes, that he's in love with the Sylph, and when she enters the clearing on the tips of her toes he can't help but be happy. He's happy until, when he holds his arm out, inviting an embrace or a pas de deux, instead of running to him or gliding to him, she keeps her distance. It's as if an electrified fence surrounded him, and she's flirting with him but she's not getting close enough to touch him, or let him touch her, and it's like the poker game, and she probably knows what will happen. He approaches her, very slowly, like approaching a frightened dog, and then he tells her, I have something for you. She sees the scarf in his hand and the magic must work because immediately she wants it, wants to hold it, to feel the fabric between her fingers. It's a gift, he says. It's my love for you. And she knows it's a mistake but she's mesmerized. She reaches out, and partly she reaches out because of the beauty of the scarf, but partly it's her desire for transformation. She wants to transform herself into a human being. If she could be human, she thinks, she could be loved, and she dances a dance full of hope, which is human, and of fear, which is also human. The Sylph must know her love is doomed but like Taglioni, when she dances she forgets what she knows, and because she believes that love is possible, when James begins moving with her, the dance they dance is the consummation of their union. When the young Nureyev holds his partner, a Russian girl, over his head, enlèvement, she's in heaven because every cell in his being is also in heaven, and after a deep arabesque, that's when she settles on the forest floor in front of him. That's when he asks her, and now she's ready to allow him, to place the scarf around her trembling form. She's nervous, and vulnerability, like nakedness, can be sexy. He slowly unfurls the scarf and drapes it over her small diaphanous wings, the wings that made her a being that couldn't be loved, and that's when the feathers of the wings, feather by feather, fall off. And there's nothing she can do. When the last feather falls to the ground she dies. And there's nothing James can do but watch the life as it fades from her face and her body, and when it's gone he's kneeling, holding her in his arms. And when the other sylphs arrive James can only watch as they lift the body of their fallen comrade and bear it up to heaven. Or *the* heavens. And James would normally make the gesture of grief but he's beyond grief. He barely notices Madge, standing behind him, not quite laughing at him but happy in her victory, what she sees as a victory. Look, she says, directing his gaze to a clearing across the forest. See what you've lost. And when he looks up he sees a wedding party, led by Effie and her new husband, Gurn, and he sees what he's lost and no one sees him. In some versions of the ballet he dies and in other versions he just collapses, but whether he's dead or almost dead, Madge always kneels over him, stroking his back like a mother, or a lover. In a version by the Royal Ballet, Madge lifts her hem, re-vealing beneath the soiled black burlap a glimpse of white tutu, as if the old witch, once upon a time, had been a sylph herself.

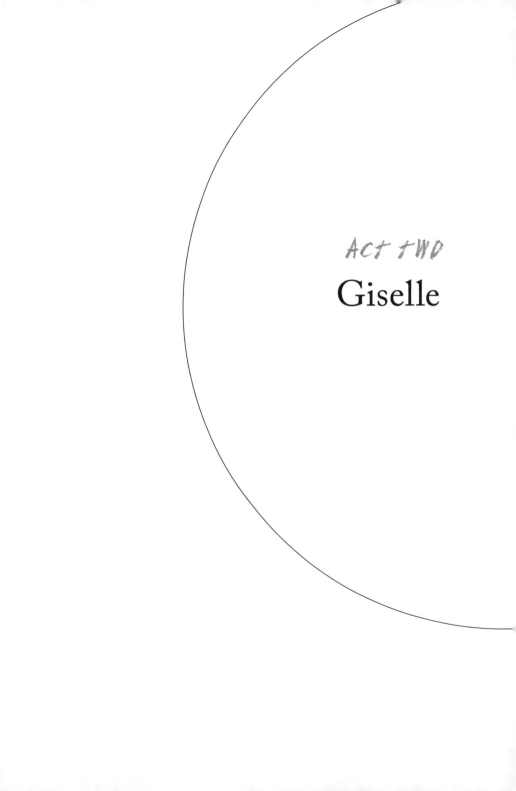

ACT TWO
Giselle

The full name of this ballet, in French, is *Giselle, ou Les Wilis*, the Wilis being a sisterhood of once-young girls who died before their wedding day. According to legend they've been cursed to rise at night and haunt, not just the men who jilted them, but all men, dancing them to their death. And although any curse, in order to work, requires belief, in the world of *Giselle* it's not a question of believing whether the Wilis exist. It's a question of how to avoid becoming one.

The curtain rises on a countryside village. A young peasant, dressed in tight pants, walks across the village square, stands in front of a particular cottage and places his open palm over his heart. This is Hilarion, the local gamekeeper, and the gesture is meant to tell us he's in love. The cottage is the cottage of Giselle, who's beautiful, and because Hilarion is awkward there's no possible way she can ever love him, which makes him first of all sad, and then angry. I say *awkward*, not because he's not a good dancer but because the gift he leaves at Giselle's door is a dead pheasant. Then a trumpet sounds, he finds a hiding place behind the village trash cans, and Albrecht appears. Albrecht is a duke, and although he has a castle somewhere, to be close to Giselle he's rented a cottage in town. He's calling himself Loys, and with the help of his squire, a dwarf named Wilfrid, he's adopted the guise of a regular villager. He goes to Giselle's front door, placing *his* open palm on his heart, and Wilfrid, who dutifully hides the royal sword and cape, has seen it all before. He's seen the elaborate seduction that leads, in the end, to some young girl getting hurt, and why the need to be constantly falling in love? Albrecht is already engaged to the daughter of a powerful prince and falling in love with a local dancer can lead to nothing but complication. But because he's a jester, all Wilfrid can do is make a joke, and when he's gone Albrecht, kicking aside the pheasant, knocks on Giselle's front door. He's been seducing Giselle long enough to know what she likes, that she likes to play games, and when she opens the door she starts dancing. This Loys fellow seems to enjoy her dancing, and she goes en pointe, showing off her technique. But Albrecht, instead of being thrilled, which he is, pretends to be uninterested. That's his game, and her part of the game is to test his sincerity. She's half teasing when she runs to a wooden bench by a fence and she's half testing when she pulls up the yellow flower growing near a fence post. Does he love me or love me not? One by one she peels off the petals, and when it gets down to three petals left Albrecht can tell how it's going to end, and to preclude that ending he pulls the flower out of her hand, crushing it with his boot. And it's not that Giselle didn't know what the flower was going to say, it's not that hard to see the future. But because she wants to believe him, when he takes her hand and very sincerely professes his love, she's happy. Part of the game is her capitulation, and when they step away from the fence they're already dancing, a pas de deux meant to express a surrendering to love, and that's when Giselle's mother appears. In Romantic ballet emotions were considered an infection, which

is why, although Berthe wants her child to experience love, because she believes in the Wilis she also believes in the danger of
love. And she's worried. They're all standing in the yard of the
cottage and Albrecht, although he may believe in Wilis theoreti-
cally, because there's nothing he can do about it, turns to Berthe
and turns on his charm. When he starts dancing with her, in a
way he's wooing her, and by wooing her he's wooing her daughter. And Berthe enjoys a kiss on the cheek, and Giselle, although
she doesn't admit it, especially to herself, watching the two of
them, feels her interest in this Loys fellow intensify. And when
eventually Albrecht turns his attention away from the mother
and back to her, that's when she realizes that she's fallen in love.
And that would be the end of the scene except that Hilarion,
having watched all this, steps out from behind his trash can.
He's wearing a hat like the one Harpo Marx used to wear, and
he's agitated, using his hat to plead with Giselle, telling her
this guy who seems so wonderful is not the person he seems to
be. He can never love you as much as I love you. But no one,
she says, is who they seem to be. She looks at Albrecht, and if
Hilarion was agitated before, now he starts to act a little crazy.
He shakes his fist at Albrecht, a gesture of hatred, a hatred aris-
ing from the image in his mind of Albrecht and Giselle making
love, an image he can't stand and can't stop seeing, and when he
curses the image, although Giselle dismisses his curse, although
she calls him a pathetic little man, when she and Albrecht walk
away, she feels a tightening across her chest.

It was very early in the morning when the poker game ended.
Seagulls were squawking out in the harbor but it was still night.
The other players had vanished, leaving Cosmo and me, and

Rachel was sorry I'd lost so much money. She seemed sad for me, as if my sadness was obvious, and Cosmo had lost money too but he often lost money. That makes it interesting, he used to say, and by *interesting* he meant risky, and at that point in my life I was willing to be risky. Rachel was putting on her coat, assuming we'd be leaving but now we were led by Freddie, the man with the large hands, into an office where another man behind a large desk seemed to be leading the proceedings. He was called the Commodore, and I say *proceedings* because it was like the sentencing phase of a trial, a trial in which Cosmo and I were found guilty of having insufficient funds. We sat in a row of chairs, Rachel between us, and the Commodore, behind his desk and behind his bushy eyebrows, was looking at pieces of paper. He asked Cosmo to sign a document, and I was told to sign a paper admitting my guilt and agreeing to repay the Commodore twenty-three thousand dollars. Which couldn't have been right. There must be a mistake. But the man who'd been the dealer, who now seemed like an accountant, showed me a bill that tallied up my loans and the total of those loans came to twenty-three thousand dollars. And maybe it was possible. Maybe I'd gotten more carried away than I thought. They seemed to have proof, and they owned the club, and Seymour, standing behind the Commodore, was staring at me as if I had no choice. So I signed my name to a contract I barely read, an agreement stipulating when I should pay them back and what might happen if I didn't pay them back, and it didn't say they would break my legs but it indicated that not making good on my loan would be bad. For me. And it was almost like a curse, you do this thing or else, and the curse was the *or else*, what might happen to me, and the funny thing was, once I'd signed the chit, and Cosmo had signed his, almost magically the mood in the room, which had been glum, became lighter, as if air was let out of a big balloon and now we could breathe. Seymour was smiling now, and the other men surrounding us were nodding, in affirmation, and Freddie patted my back and Cosmo shook hands with the various men and I shook hands with the Commodore, his thick knuckles wrapped around my thin knuckles, and it all seemed amiable enough until I thought about what I had signed.

Before I lived in Los Angeles I lived with a woman in Chicago. We'd met, fallen in love, and I thought love, and specifically my loving another person, would lead to a life I could be happy with. And mostly I was, but the thing that would draw me to Cosmo was in me then, my desire to have a better, and therefore different life, and then we had a child, a girl. The circle of love we had seemed to grow, and it did, and the problem was the expectation it would continue to grow. Victor Hugo, who wrote the poem that inspired *Giselle*, also wrote a play. *Le roi s'amuse*. It's the basis of the opera *Rigoletto*, about a court jester, a hunchback with a large face who loves his child, an adolescent girl, and my daughter was never an adolescent but I know what he wanted, to protect his daughter, which meant controlling what happened to her, and you can't control everything. His day job consisted of ridiculing the men whose wives and daughters had been seduced by his boss, and the story is a comedy until one of these men lays a curse on Rigoletto. It's a father's curse, and Rigoletto is used to curses but because his love for his daughter is absolutely complete, this curse sticks to him. And I didn't know if I ever had a curse laid on me but I remember watching my daughter, on her blue scooter, scooting along on the sidewalk in front of me, and she was a cautious person but don't take your eyes off her for an instant, that's what I told my wife and she told me but all it took was that one time she didn't stop at the corner, and it was like a curse.

We drove Rachel back to her house and Cosmo, being a gentleman, escorted her up the steep concrete steps to her door. He had Rachel on one arm, a bottle of champagne cradled in the other, and he told me to follow him. Which I did. I noticed the sky beginning to lighten up, and Cosmo had told me to lighten up in the car, to let what had happened be over, and it was over, a done deal, but because I had lost a lot of money the adrenaline of what had happened was still inside me. Rachel was tired, I could tell, and when Rachel's mother, wearing a yellow dress with pink flowers, appeared on the porch she didn't invite us in but Cosmo didn't need an invitation. You're looking beautiful, he said, and everyone wants to be beautiful, and when he kissed her cheek she smiled and suddenly we were inside the house. And this is part of why I wanted to imitate Cosmo. He made people happy. He set the champagne on the kitchen table, and when Rachel went to her room to change clothes, and since he'd had more than a few drinks, he took Betty's hand. He lifted her arm, and it was more like a representation of dancing, what they did, not really dancing, although music was playing, a Frank Sinatra–type song, and he twirled her like actual dancing and whatever it was gave her pleasure. She was older than Cosmo but not by much, and as Cosmo flirted with her, and she with him, I could almost see her growing younger, her lips full, her eyes sparkling, and because she wasn't young she probably appreciated the attention, which was Cosmo's specialty, focusing on a person and bathing that person in the heat of his attention, which is why I was watching him, to learn his technique. Although it was more than technique. The radio song was a song he knew, and he wasn't singing the words but he was talking them, swirling Betty across the kitchen, his hand on her hip and a smile on his face, a smile meant for her but also for me, a smile of complicity and joy, and the reason for joy is that someone was feeling emotion. And where would that go? In his black tuxedo he was elegant but slightly debauched, elegant because a tuxedo is elegant and debauched because his bow tie was hanging to one side. When he suggested popping the champagne cork Betty was giggling like a girl, or like a woman being swept away from herself. Being the object of his interest felt good, and his heat felt good, and I couldn't hear what he whispered in her ear, and the words didn't matter because what mattered was the fact of his breath, brushing past her downy ear hairs, bypassing the brain which would have told her that this man, with his shaven cheeks, his thick hair, his sly smile, was here for her daughter. He found four cocktail glasses, filled them, passed one to me and one to Betty, and then holding his by the stem, spiraled his arms around Betty's arm. They took sips from the rim and naturally some champagne was spilled, but they didn't notice because they were laughing. And when Rachel opened her bedroom door, wearing a floral robe tied at the waist, he seamlessly transitioned between mother and daughter, giving Betty a kiss on her cheek as he took Rachel's hand, kissing her hand like a knight might kiss a lady's hand, or like a knight-errant, on an errand or in error, and whatever it was I could see the power of Cosmo's attention. Rachel was smiling, and because his adoration of Rachel implied an adoration of the woman who created

Rachel, Betty was smiling too. And it wasn't just women who received the gift of his focus. I was also included, happy to be pulled into the circle of, I want to say love but it was just a circle of feeling, and mostly Cosmo was at the center but sometimes Rachel, and I felt it too. And I wanted more. Which is why, although the city was lit up outside the picture window, I wasn't looking out the window. I was watching Cosmo, craving a magnetism I knew was rooted in his need to be loved, like a thirst, and this is what he did to satisfy that thirst.

Giselle's mother is charmed by this fellow called Loys because Albrecht, acting the part of Loys, is charming. Berthe makes it easy for him to seduce Giselle. Like any Casanova, Albrecht gets his pleasure from the process of seduction, the figuring out how this particular girl needs to be coaxed and led, and in a way massaged, into a willingness to submit. The first thing Albrecht does is gather information, talking to her friends and her mother, finding out what she likes and dislikes, and he uses her gestures when he talks to her, and her tone of voice, and naturally she trusts someone who, in ways she's not even aware of, seems to be like her. And for Albrecht, the art of it isn't just seeming to be like her, he actually, as much as he can, becomes her, and although he doesn't dance on point, he does dance on the balls of his feet, and in this way, to a certain extent, he becomes more like a woman. And if the dancer who dances Albrecht is good, you can see his center of gravity change, his chest expand, and in Nureyev's version of Albrecht, when he walks across the town square, his hips swaying like a woman's hips, or a girl's, it's not that he's dancing in a feminine way because what is that? There is no feminine way. But he's being something other than what he is, transforming himself, and if he's good, like Nureyev dancing with Margot Fonteyn, you can't help watching him. You can't help following his lead because his dancing expresses a real joy, and the place he's leading her is where she already wants to go. That was Nureyev's skill, understanding desire and then making himself the object of desire.

Cosmo was pouring champagne, saying *fantastic* as he ceremoniously lifted his glass. He didn't specify what was fantastic, or why, but there was always a toast with Cosmo. To love, or sadness. And I assumed that after a drink we'd go back to the car but Cosmo pulled out a kitchen chair for Betty to sit. He was in an expansive mood, and although Rachel wasn't enjoying it as much as Betty, they both sat at the kitchen table. And I did too, next to Cosmo, who was facing the two of them, and he didn't just compliment people. He actually was interested in what they thought and felt, and what they didn't even know they felt. Maybe that's why we never talked about my daughter. It wasn't a secret, but secrets make us who we are, that's what he said one time, and for Cosmo, the conundrum was, once he knew a person's secrets he got bored. And it wasn't that what he said was so interesting, but the three of us were all facing him, our eyes and ears directed at him, and attention is a kind of love, and he was taking it in. I'd known Cosmo about a year, about as long as I'd been in L.A., and it wasn't just charm because charm is easy. Watching him I could see the charm, but below the charm there was intensity, and below that there was heat, and maybe it was a metaphorical heat but it was coming from him, like a fire burning itself, and we could all feel it. Ladies, he said, and turning to me, gentleman, and he pushed back his chair, and then he walked off to find the bathroom. The way he did even that was charming. And when he'd gone the three of us were left looking at each other. I was trying not to think about the money I owed, which for me was an inconceivable amount of money, and because it was inconceivable I was able to push those thoughts from my mind. Or at least I tried. But the conversation we had, the three of us, sitting at the table, always came back to silence because what can you say? Without Cosmo nothing much got said. And because of the metaphorical heat he'd been generating before, not only was the silence noticeable, it was slightly uncomfortable. Betty's hands were folded on the table and Rachel was looking off to the living room. I would look at her and then look down at the parabolic designs on the table, trying to find the pattern in what first appeared like random shapes, and the same design was on the upholstery of the chair, the empty chair that Cosmo had been sitting on. And it was more an impulse than an actual idea, but I followed the impulse and slid from my chair, across the space between the chairs, to the chair Cosmo had been sitting on. And any time you sit on a chair that's been occupied by someone, there's always a little residual heat. And maybe it was my imagination but this seemed hotter than residual heat, and I felt it rising up from the chair into me. I was sitting fairly straight, my sitting bones absorbing my weight, and when I looked over at Rachel, instead of letting her look away, I said something. I don't know what, and it doesn't matter because I just started paying attention. There was Rachel, and Betty was next to her, and I was talking to Rachel, not like Cosmo would talk but I seemed to be engaging both of them, as if not just Cosmo's heat but his charisma was radiating up from the padded vinyl and radiating into me, as if part of him, the glowing part, was entering me. The physical sensation of my muscles, relaxed and loose, and my bones, supported by my muscles, was enjoyable, and the ability to be the center of a conversation, that was also enjoyable. And if it would have been just enjoyment I would have wanted it to go on forever. But rising up through the padded seat, into the cheeks of my butt and the bones of my butt and up through my organs and into my heart, along with the heat was a feeling of need. Although I could feel my lips smiling, and Rachel was smiling back at me, and Betty was laughing and I was laughing and in a way it was all good, in another way the intensity was making me nervous. Pleasure was on one side, and anxiety was on the same side, and I was experiencing both of them, in my mind and body, and as I did I noticed the heat begin to dissipate. I noticed a few more caesuras, as they say, in the conversation, which was getting less interesting to me and probably to Rachel and Betty, and I was trying not to think about money, trying to imagine a mind that can bear to keep burning when Cosmo stepped up to the table. And when he sat down in the empty chair, the one that had been mine, almost immediately we turned toward him. Like heliotropic plants, except we weren't plants, we were human, and I did it too, *Cosmotropic*, turning toward him because that's where the life was. Our thoughts turned, and our desires turned, and the heat I'd been feeling so intensely was now just a warmth, if that, and it didn't take long before the champagne bottles were empty, and when Cosmo stood up we all stood up, and down at the bottom of the steep concrete steps, at the curb, the limousine was waiting.

I was older than my wife but it didn't seem to matter. Desire doesn't really care about the object of desire, it cares about itself. She didn't know what love was any more than I did, but we believed it could be trained, almost like a muscle, developed in each other to focus on each other, and because we were young and we thought we could be anything we wanted, we thought of ourselves as happy. I pretended to be who I was, and she appeared to be who she was, and in the beginning there were some adjustments but the more I gave her my desire, in the form of attention, which was sincere because I did desire her, the more the desire was kindled in her, and who knows, we thought, maybe this is love. And those thoughts of love began to connect us, to bind our bodies and the cells that lived and died and made our bodies, and because we were skeptics, we dismissed it, but because we were human we believed that our happiness would go on forever.

Carlotta Grisi originated the role of Giselle in 1841, and since then every great ballerina, as a way to measure her greatness, has taken it on. It's a role that requires acting, but what the great ballerinas have is not just an ability to act the part of a girl in love but to *be* a girl in love and let those feelings express themselves in dance. Crossing the line between acting love and feeling the actual surge of that love in the body was something Grisi must have done because she fell in love with the man who created, in the story he wrote, the role of Albrecht. And the great Anna Pavlova must have felt it as strongly as anyone. Haskell tells us: *With Pavlova there can be no other word than genius. To have seen her in nothing [other than in* Giselle*] is to have seen every facet of her art.* Haskell is dead, as is anyone who saw Pavlova dance, but we assume that when she danced Giselle she became the innocent young girl who, in her first experience of love, believes that love and life are synonymous. *What struck me*, Haskell says, *was not just the fact that her dancing seemed entirely spontaneous, but that it* *seemed a natural phenomenon, like the ripple of a pond, the opening of the flower, or the leaves being whisked and whirled by the wind.* I've seen videos of Pavlova dancing and I'm not as impressed as Haskell. Partly it's the quality of the video, but partly it's the style of her dancing, as if she's doing an impression of a ballerina, waving her arms in the delicate arc we expect to see from a ballerina. So it must have been her physical presence. Being in front of a living human being who radiated heat, I know what that's like, and *passion* is a word, but what she felt, and therefore what she expressed, transcended words and even images. Which is why Haskell sounds like a man in love when, describing her, he says *her long, perfectly proportioned arms accentuated the large noble movements of the Russian school, while her well-modeled legs, her strong slender ankles, and her highly developed instep gave her pointes a unique beauty. Her face was not beautiful; it was more than that. It could assume beauty at will, so that there was not one Pavlova, but many.*

Pavlova was born into poverty in 1881, and her rise into the ranks of the great ballerinas had as much to do with tenacity as natural ability. She studied with Petipa in St. Petersburg and danced for Diaghilev in Paris, and her history is the history of Romantic ballet. But her fame, the reason Haskell fell in love with her, was because she wanted to dance for herself. Like Dickens on tour with his novels, she went on tour with her ballet, in Europe and America, anywhere she was asked to go. She performed sections of the great ballets for people who had never seen ballet, and because she was romantic, she believed the world could be perfect, and because she was a dancer she tried to express that perfect world. Balanchine said that to be romantic about something is to see what you are and to wish for something entirely different. It's a kind of magical thinking that let Pavlova believe she could feel, not just what Giselle was feeling because most people can do that, most people have a memory of some version of love, but calling that up, night after night, and her version must have been intense. She must have wanted love and also feared love, and because of that fear it was easy for her to believe in the curse of the Wilis, those spirits that rise at night and terrorize men. They're led by Myrtha, the so-called queen of the Wilis, but more on her later.

Now it's grape harvest time in the village. The peasants gather around Giselle and everyone dances with her. Albrecht does, his arms around her thin waist, and when the couples split apart and new couples join together, that's when Hilarion takes Giselle by the hand, and when he dances with her, supporting her arabesque, what he's doing is the same thing I did when I tried to imitate Cosmo. Hilarion is imitating Albrecht, trying to be someone who can partner Giselle by attracting her attention and keeping her attention. If you lack a trait, assume it, that's what Shakespeare said, and Hilarion is trying to generate the same heat that Albrecht generates, a heat that Giselle will feel and be attracted to, but like me trying to be Cosmo, it doesn't work. And when the couples pair off again, this time with Albrecht partnering Giselle, it's obvious where the love is because Albrecht, an experienced lover, knows how to make a space for love. He's danced with enough girls to be confident, and his confidence becomes part of his charm, and he knows how to lift Giselle and balance her, and the other dancers stand back to watch. Hilarion watches too, until he can't stand it anymore. His attempt to be Albrecht didn't work, he thinks, because Albrecht is false, and I'm not false and I won't be. He steps into the middle of the pas de deux, breaking it up and pulling Giselle in a way that almost trips her, and he warns her again not to trust that man, but that man is the man she loves, and if there's any feeling of competition, Albrecht doesn't show it. He invites Hilarion to hop on the wagon he commandeers, a wagon filled with the harvest of grapes and there's wine, and no one questions why he passes out glasses of wine because belief is blinding. Giselle is blinded by what seems to her the inevitability of her love. They drop Hilarion off at his cottage, a ramshackle cottage at the edge of the village, and as he watches them drive away he knows the next part of the story is undanced, the part when they make love. It's undanced because when the two of them, on a picnic blanket, take off their tights, it isn't necessarily graceful. Giselle lets him pull the stretchy material down over her thin ankles, getting caught on her thin white shoes, and they laugh as their naked bodies entwine.

One cannot and should not rule out sex from ballet. For some types of mind the sex appeal of the dancers may be an inducement to visit the ballet. Haskell, in his own way, is talking about the sexuality that exists, and has to exist, when watching nearly naked people, beautiful nearly naked people, perform. It's possible to sit so far away that the bodies of the dancers, the thighs and breasts and buttocks all flatten out. I've had seats up there, in the upper balconies, and I know ballet isn't a strip show, but I know the closer you sit the more you feel the intimacy, or the more I feel it, and that intimacy is part of the sexuality, which is part of what keeps pulling me back to the dancing. Human beings, on display, in their tights and leotards. And in the old days the material wasn't as clingy as it is now but even then you would've seen, very clearly, what the muscles of the bodies of the dancers were doing. One time Nijinsky, dancing for some royalty in Russia, had to stop dancing because whatever he was wearing to cover his penis didn't cover enough. That's the story anyway, and it's believable because the whole reason for wearing tights is to show the muscles, and sometimes they're bulging muscles. The quadriceps, in male dancers, are especially developed. And the gluteus. And the girls. And *for some types of mind* it's the ballerinas, their ribs rising and falling with the exertion of dancing, an exertion that makes them hot, and if you sit close enough, you can see the sweat on their brows, and their armpits are wet, and the gluteus muscle is one of the largest muscles in the body. Margot Fonteyn, although she was no longer a girl, when she danced with Rudolph Nureyev, by presenting herself in the role of someone young and pliable, excited desire in a lot of people. Youth is beautiful, and a dancer's body is trained to be flexible and strong, and even if it's not actually naked, it's possible to fall in love with a naked dancer's body because the nakedness exists in the imagination, where it has its power.

The actual job I had when I first met Cosmo, the one that paid me, was at a telephone answering service in Hollywood. It was located in a small office on Ivar Street, and people would call, leave messages for people, and those people would call to find out what the messages were. Most of our clients were in the industry, that's what people called it, actors usually, struggling probably, and my job was to relay information about meetings and casting calls. Businesses like that don't exist anymore, and even back then it was sometimes slow. I had time to read books, look at magazines, and mainly I just stared into space. The pay wasn't terrible but I would never even get close to saving up twenty-three thousand dollars. And my friends didn't have that kind of money. My ex-wife, my relatives, they were all distant or dead. I could probably have scraped together a thousand dollars, maybe two, and one idea I had, in lieu of paying back my debt, was to make myself scarce. Out of sight is out of mind, that's what they say, but even if that were true, which I don't think it is, the men I borrowed the money from were not the kind of people to forget about me. I know I hadn't forgotten about them. I could feel them, like a band of tension extending down from the back of my skull, knotting up my trapezius, and whatever tension was causing the knot, I didn't want it stuck in me because I didn't want to stick it in my clients. The people I massaged. For free. A man named Daryl had answered one of my ads, and as I drove home, down Rowena, I was trying to mentally prepare myself, imagining the fibers in the back of my neck elongating and softening, and when I pulled into my driveway, parked in the space where Juan let me park, I thought I felt a little more relaxed. It was in this state of relative relaxation that I performed the ritual, inside my house, of opening my massage table, laying out the sheets, putting the pillow in a pillowcase, and it was important, when my doorbell rang, that my money troubles become a thing of the past. If I was thinking about ways to come up with twenty-three thousand dollars I couldn't concentrate on Daryl, who arrived, took off his shoes, and his eyes reminded me of a squirrel. He was about thirty, his hair in a ponytail, and he presented, as they say, with a problem in his hip, a lack of mobility that was obvious. Once he got down to his underwear I had him stretch out on the table, on his back, and because he was skinny I could see his musculature and through that to his skeleton and I saw that one leg, his right, was shorter than the other.

This shorter leg would need to be released, and I intended to do that by loosening the tendons that held the femur into the hip. But because those tendons are small, and because they're buried under larger tendons and protected by larger muscles, the first step was to wake them up. Once they woke up I could start relaxing them. Muscles need to be relaxed to do their jobs, and so starting at the surface, I began working in from the superficial muscles, softening them until the fluids began to flow, and by *fluids* I mean not just blood. The Chinese have several names for the current that runs through the body and that's what I planned to set free. *Set free* is probably too ambitious, but creating a little space in the hip socket, that I could do. Starting with his foot, I worked my way up his calf, following the contour of muscle as it winds its way around the bone, spiraling up around the knee. The quadriceps and hamstrings and the tender adductors are all connected to the pelvis, and to understand the muscle I needed, in a way, to become the muscle. And I thought I was doing a pretty good job until the image of the men at the gambling parlor, and the one with the mustache especially, Seymour, entered my brain. And the minute it did I could feel Daryl's body stiffen, which meant that I'd stiffened, and when I dove back into his body, into the current moving through his flesh, my hands extending out of my body, I was listening to his body telling me where the current was dammed, like a beaver dam, and it wasn't easy, but by imagining the muscle fibers and even the cells inside those fibers, I would break the dam and get rid of the image of Seymour.

The village is empty except for Hilarion. He's peeping into the window of Albrecht's cottage, stepping inside the unlocked door as the wedding party comes into view. Bathilde, the bride-to-be,

and her father, the prince, drive up to the town square. Gradually
the entire village begins to assemble and the prince, who's thirsty,
calls for refreshments. Where's Albrecht, he wants to know.
Wilfrid steps out from the crowd to explain that the groom-to-be
has been detained, that he's still at the church, praying. Giselle's
mother has been hired to cater the wedding and Giselle is the one
who brings out the wine and everyone drinks. Giselle, because
she's the best dancer in the village, dances for the royal guests,
and because her performance impresses Bathilde, after it's over
the two girls sit together, talking. Giselle admires the fabric of
Bathilde's dress and Bathilde admires Giselle's beauty. They sit
on a bench talking about dancing and jewelry, and Giselle tells
Bathilde she's in love with a man. And since they're both in love,
although they don't know it's the same man, they talk and laugh,
and Bathilde, feeling generous, gives Giselle a necklace. As a
way to thank her, Giselle executes a brief pirouette, whirling
around on the point of one foot, an invitation for everyone to
join in a dance, which they do. Bathilde dances with her father,
an oddly intimate dance in which the father seems more lover
than father, and at the end of it the father and daughter are offered one of the cottages, so that they can take a nap. Wilfrid
signals with his horn that it's safe for Albrecht, and when he arrives Giselle performs a series of demi-pliés and relevés leading up to a large jeté, a jump into Albrecht's arms. Because it's
a ballet, the wedding guests, who temporarily stopped dancing,
start again, and it's like a scene out of Breughel. The whole village has joined in the celebration, everyone dancing or drinking
wine, and Giselle's mother is trying to catch her daughter to slow
her down. She's worried about the Wilis, about what might happen if her delicate daughter exerts herself too much, and what if

she dies before her wedding day? And although Giselle is high strung, or because she is, she pushes herself, enjoying Albrecht and enjoying the enjoyment of him, and her mother begs her to stop but she refuses to believe there's a price to pay.

Every muscle has learned to express itself, and the problem is, in some cases, they've learned the wrong lesson. Imagine if you were born on a hillside and spent your entire life walking on the hillside. If all you knew was the incline of the hill, your sense of level would be corrupted. Your muscles would become so accustomed to the angle of the hill that retraining those muscles would require retraining your memories, and because memories, like people, want to be comfortable, and since it took time for them to learn what comfortable was, to change the idea of comfortable takes time. And attention. Which is why I had Daryl, my client, turn onto his stomach. His muscles were working in the way they'd been taught, and I began by trying to unteach the ones that connected the femur to the pelvis, not coercing them but coaxing them into length. Just a little at a time, hoping not to attract attention to what I was doing because, although awareness is usually good, in this case I wanted to circumvent awareness, distracting both his muscle and his mind, and let the muscle adjust itself. I found a bony protuberance near his sitting bone, and I didn't know the names of the tendons down there but I felt them with my thumb, and using my thumb I pressed in, and my hand had gotten strong, and I pressed in hard. I could feel him respond, first with tension, which I told him to let go of, then with his attempt at letting go, and although I was telling him to relax, at the same time I wanted him to feel what I was doing because while he was feeling that, which probably felt like pain, I was doing other things. I was using my knuckle to dig in through the sheath of muscle, to the fascia holding those muscles in place, urging them to expand and extend. And I could hear his shallow breathing. I was listening to his body, and his body was leading me to this one particular tendon, attached to the bone like a limpet attached to a rock, and I was following the guidance of his body, and just about when I was ready to apply the pressure I'd been waiting to apply, that's when Seymour appeared again. In my image of him he had his hand out, and I told Daryl to take a deep breath. I dismissed the idea of money from my mind, and all my ideas, turning my focus to a point inside the sacrum where nerve and skeleton come together, and Seymour's mustache was thick and blond, and I was seeing the variegated hairs of that mustache as I pressed the spot I'd searched for and found, and the spot was the right spot, and because it was right Daryl screamed. And because pain can be part of the process I kept pressing. And it wasn't the screaming that stopped me, it was his arm, reaching back, smacking at the side of my head. Daryl rolled off the table and landed in a crouch. The table was about four feet off the floor and he was bent over, holding his sacrum, looking back at his butt and then at me, and when I asked him if he felt any pain he told me I was a fucking idiot. You fucking shit. Fuck you, fuck you, and obviously he was in pain. Which I didn't intend. Although I did. And I told him I was sorry. When I offered to massage the area to ease the pain he called me a fucking asshole. He was able to stand, and he was on one side of the table and I was on the other, and I could tell he didn't want me anywhere near him. His right leg, the one I'd been working on, was bent, but he was able to limp to the chair, get his pants over his legs, and he was speaking, but not to me.

He was speaking about me. Talking briefly about legal issues but mainly about how he'd like to make me feel the pain he was feeling. Which was natural. And it was natural, once he got dressed, that the feeling he was feeling became less acute. I didn't say anything because I knew he was angry but when he opened the door, as a way to normalize our relationship, which shouldn't have been jeopardized by an experience that might, in the end, turn out to be beneficial, I asked him if he wanted to make an appointment for the following week. He didn't even say fuck you this time. He just walked out, limping slightly, and as I watched him limp down my driveway I noticed a car at the curb. I couldn't see who was driving, but the man who was sitting in the passenger side opened the door and there was Seymour, smiling, pulling at his mustache. He waved when he saw me, walked up the driveway, and between each apartment was a narrow concrete patio, and I had a plastic table, two chairs, a succulent plant inherited from the former tenant, and I kept my motor scooter there. It was a Slovenian moped I kept locked to some pipes by the house, and Seymour sat on one of my plastic chairs. He was smoking a cigarette. The table was green, with two matching chairs, and when he finished his smoke he stood up, shorter than I was, and he said he'd like to see my place. Meaning the inside of my house. And why do you need to come inside? He didn't say anything but I followed him around to my door, and it wasn't necessary to invite him in because I was following him in. Nice place, he said, looking around. I had a desk and a sofa and the chairs were pushed aside to make the massage area, and he looked at the table and at a painting on my wall, and without looking at me he walked into the kitchen. He seemed to like the kitchen. Nice tile, he said, and he lit a burner on the stove to light another cigarette. And I might've accepted his offer of a cigarette except for the fact that he wasn't asking me to take one, he was telling me. And even if I owed his boss some money, I thought of myself as an independent operator, and I told him I was fine. And he said, that's good. Because we were wondering. If you've made any headway. And I knew what he was talking about and I told him, I'm working on it. He nodded, both suspicious and approving, and what I noticed about Seymour was his big smile. And the specific thing I noticed about his big smile was its falseness. Or seeming falseness. It seemed false to me because it seemed so easy. And maybe it was easy, maybe he'd been gifted with cheek muscles that easily slid his lips across his teeth in what they call a winning smile. Or maybe he worked at it. Maybe Seymour, like a weight lifter, had developed a set of smile muscles that let him, like a strongman pressing a barbell over his head, press his smile. It didn't seem to grow out of amusement or mirth. It just appeared on his face, and like a weight lifter, once he'd lifted it, he dropped it. And I thought about offering him tea or coffee but then he'd have to stay, and I had nothing of value so I wasn't worried about him stealing anything or breaking anything, but the fact that I was thinking about him breaking something got me worried. Like an appraiser he roamed from the kitchen into my bedroom, wiping his finger along the base of my lamp as if looking for dust, and when he patted the head of a happy-face–sad-face mask on my wall I felt an impulse to protect the face from what he was about to do. Which was nothing. He was friendly. He asked me about my day, about work, and I wasn't thinking about Cosmo, but Cosmo would probably tell him a story, and I started talking about work, about Mike Conners, which wasn't really a story but Mike Conners was the star of a television show called *Mannix*. He used the answering service, and sometimes I'd talk to him to give him his messages. And Seymour must have seen the show, a detective show, because he seemed slightly impressed that I got to talk to a television star. He didn't spend much time in my bathroom which was connected to another room, a small bedroom that I used as both a closet and a place to keep my bicycle. He placed his hand on the saddle of the bike and asked me, You ride this? And I was trying to give him the impression that he was welcome, that he could stay in my house as long as he wanted, thinking that if he thought I wanted him to leave he wouldn't leave, and I was hoping he would finish his tour of my house but he seemed interested in the bike. It wasn't a great bike but the derailleurs were good and the brakes were good, and by now the cigarette he'd lit in the kitchen was down to the filter, and as he sucked on it he was looking at me and he must have seen some tension in my face because he told me to relax. You wear a helmet, right? But first of all, I didn't want to relax, and second, I didn't like people telling me how to be, or what I should do, and mainly I didn't want him in my house. And it wasn't his comment about a helmet that agitated me. It was the money I owed. My life was moving in a certain direction, a direction I admit might not have been the best direction, but it was my direction, a direction I'd chosen, and I didn't want to give him the power to alter that direction or alter me, and why should I change direction for this guy? Then he took a last drag of his cigarette, stubbed it out on a plastic plate, a green and yellow plate that had been my daughter's, pressing the still red ember into the green plastic, which melted enough to absorb the cigarette, and he left it sticking up like a cactus, or a tumor, and then he leaned over the handlebars of the bike. He pretended to rev it up. How fast does it go? Not very, I told him, and he told me I didn't look very fast, and then, gripping the brakes of the bike as if he was descending a steep alpine road he said, you need good brakes. And I agreed that brakes were crucial, and he said, no, I'm telling you. The brakes are what keep you from, if a car comes out of nowhere, boom! And I knew what he meant so I nodded. You know what I mean? Yes, I said, and he shook his head. The human body. It's an amazing instrument, right? But imagine a bicycle coming one way and a car coming the other way, and with his hands moving in the air in front of his chest he demonstrated the slow-motion coming together of two moving objects. We're fragile animals, he said. Without protection the bones of the body are like . . . and he winced, thinking of bones penetrating skin, and teeth shattering, and I was thinking the same thing and then he laughed. Not a real laugh. But that won't happen to you, right? You've got good brakes. And I realized that Seymour's attitude of friendliness was in direct proportion to the sense of threat he exuded. The nicer he was the scarier he was, and he was being extremely nice. His words were. But something was lurking behind his words, like his smile lurking behind his mustache, and I didn't put my finger on what it was until he told me he liked me. You're funny, he said. You're a funny guy, and then with his hand he tousled my hair, as if tousling the hair of a child except I wasn't a child and I found it demeaning. It was more like rubbing, what he did, rubbing his hand on my scalp a little harder than he needed to, and then he said, hasta la vista. And when he walked to the door I didn't say it to his face, but I walked with him down the steps to the driveway, and when he told me he'd be seeing me later, that's when I said it, loud enough to hear inside my head. Asshole. And although he didn't break anything or take anything or hang around very long, once he was gone, instead of feeling relief, I felt the opposite of relief, not fear exactly, but I knew what these guys were capable of doing, and intimidation was only part of it. For intimidation to work they needed to back it up now and then with violence. I watched him walk down the driveway, open the large door of the gold Cadillac, and then I turned and walked back to my front-door steps. I knew I was being watched, and although I didn't want to perform, and didn't know what it was I was performing, when I opened my door and stepped inside my house, that's what I was doing.

There are two basic ways to change a situation. One is to change the situation, and the other is to change how you respond to the situation. Hilarion, the gamekeeper, was attempting the former. The wedding festivities are happening on the town square and Hilarion is inside Albrecht's cottage. It's supposedly Loys's cottage, but Hilarion doesn't believe that and now he finds the royal sword lying on the bed, the royal red cape is hanging on a hook, and he knows that Loys isn't Loys, that he's a duke who's engaged to be married. Holding the sword in one hand, the cape in the other, he walks out of the cottage and when he steps into the middle of the happy dancing he's hard to ignore. He's yelling, first of all. And it's almost a yell of joy because now he has his proof. He throws the sword in front of Giselle and shows her the cape to show she's about to make a big mistake but now she doesn't have to. You see, he says, and he tells Giselle her lover is a liar. And what is that, she says. A word you made up? It means nothing to me because I don't believe it. But here's the proof, he says, and although the story happens at a time when objects had power, she refuses to accept that power. It could be anyone's sword. And because words also had power then, the way to find the truth was to ask the person who might not be telling the truth. Ask him what his name is, find out if he's really the person he pretends to be. Well that's easy enough. She sweeps her leg in front of her, in a ballet move called développé, and she does it as if sweeping away all the confusion. She asks Albrecht if all this, meaning all this ridiculousness, is true. And because words had power, he didn't dare lie. He didn't even think of lying. Or if he did, it felt pointless. He says nothing, but the questions keep coming, and finally yes, he admits it, he's not Loys. And did you love me, she wants to know. And he did, and does still. And he's trying to explain how that might happen when Giselle starts to break down, her life on the one hand, and her reason for life on the same hand, suddenly not existing. He's basically telling her the love they had, a love she felt and knew was real, wasn't real, and you can say to someone, you'll get over it, eventually, but Giselle can't get over it. She doesn't speak. And this is why Pavlova was so good in the role. She could inhabit the moment when the intimation of madness begins to flicker behind the eyes.

A Woman Under the Influence is a movie made by John Cassavetes. It's about a woman named Mabel, a wife and mother, and it's clear from the film that her madness is not entirely self-induced. Gena Rowlands plays Mabel and Peter Falk is the husband, a man who doesn't understand what's happening to his wife. He sees her being inappropriate, talking nonsense and talking to strangers, and the reasons for her inappropriateness are the influences she's under. The love she thought was permanent suddenly isn't, and as her security falls away she becomes more and more desperate to connect with her husband and children, and that desperation pushes her, and pushes them, farther away. She thinks she's acting in a sensible way, and in the movie you can see her trying to be as honest as she can, with herself and them, honestly acting out feelings that arise in her but people don't want honesty. Her kids do. And we do. We see her madness as a reasonable response to a situation that has no reasonable response, and when she's institutionalized in a hospital we feel an injustice has been done. But at the same time she is crazy. The movie is set in Los Angeles, and I can recognize some of the places she goes, one of the bars. She drinks too much, and that adds to her problems, and when she comes home from the hospital she's very subdued. Her extended family is there, all of them urging her, and wanting her, to demonstrate her sanity. Her husband demands that she be herself but every time she tries to be herself he shuts her up. A numbness has swollen her once-expressive face, and in her effort to act out normality she holds on to that numbness, but the numbness starts breaking down. There's a moment when she turns to her father. The family is sitting at a large table and he's at the other end of the table and she looks up and quietly asks him to stand up for her. Her father hesitates, then literally stands, pushes back his chair, and what do you want me to do, he says. And we know what she wants him to do, and we would do it, and when he refuses to do it there's nothing left but go crazy.

George Balanchine is considered one of the greatest choreographers of the twentieth century. I remember seeing one of his abstract ballets, they were often abstract, and being mesmerized, not by any one dancer but by the form that was made when all of them danced together. Balanchine lived ballet and was the champion, during his reign as ballet master for the New York City Ballet, of a number of great ballerinas. But near the end of his life he had health problems. He was in his seventies when he started showing signs of a disease, some unknown disease that was later found to be Creutzfeldt-Jakob disease. It's a neurological disorder, and one way to get it is to come in contact with animals, the spinal fluid of animals. And one of the symptoms is that you start to go crazy. Balanchine noticed, in the beginning, a slight unsteadiness, but anyone who gets old gets unsteady. And he adjusted. Instead of demonstrating what he wanted his dancers to do, instead of pirouetting or jumping or looking into the eyes of a ballerina, he had to tell them what he wanted. Later, his vision got blurry. It got difficult for him to see the stage. Even with glasses he couldn't see the details in the dance, and because his art was about the details it worried him. He saw doctors, but they could find nothing wrong, high blood pressure maybe, or a bad heart—but it wasn't his heart. And gradually, as the disease ate away at his neurological functioning he had less and less physical ability, and then less mental ability, and because making dances was his life he kept doing it, but since his balance was bad he had to use a cane, which was embarrassing for him, so he used to walk with an umbrella. It became part of his costume. Even on sunny days. And inside the ballet studio he would have to sit or lean against a wall, and people could see what was happening but no one mentioned it. When he took a curtain call he held the curtain to help himself stand, and it wasn't just balance. After his eyesight began to fail, then his hearing did. Music, which was the pulse of his choreography, wasn't his to enjoy anymore. And it kept getting worse, or he did, getting dizzier and less focused, feeling not just old, but dying, and he *was* dying, but he was still a young man in his mind, still virile, or at least virile in his way, but that's not true. He wasn't virile, and that was a fact that played on his vanity. He was a personality. People came to the ballet to see how he used ballet to say what he wanted to say and now, first of all, he couldn't even see what he'd done, and second, he couldn't do what he used to do. He couldn't see colors so he couldn't design the lights for his dances, and yes, he had eye operations and heart operations, and he believed in the power of medicine but now he was getting confused. He didn't remember things. Obvious things. Who is that person talking to me, and how did I get this fork in my hand. It got harder and harder to hold the fork, and sometimes he fell down, but he could get back up because he didn't want to give in. Getting old isn't fun, and for him, an ex-dancer, with people watching him to learn his dances and seeing him deteriorate, it was intolerable. It was difficult, given his clumsiness, to be George Balanchine, and then his language started to go. He lost the use of English, his adopted language, and then, even in Russian he could no longer communicate with people. And gradually, he could no longer communicate with himself, which is a definition of madness, the inability to remember who you are and why you are, and gradually the emptiness of that gets filled, and we call them hallucinations but it's the mind's attempt, or the soul's, no longer able to connect with itself, but trying, and in the end, in the hospital, he couldn't even swallow. What he died of, officially, was pneumonia, but when an autopsy was finally performed on his brain, when they sliced his brain into thin layers, under a microscope they discovered the abnormalities of Creutzfeldt-Jakob.

What finally breaks Giselle's heart happens when Bathilde emerges from the cottage, refreshed from her nap, and seeing Albrecht, runs to him. Giselle watches, nearly catatonic, her friends at her side as this other girl embraces the man she loves. The man who loves her. And because Albrecht actually does love Giselle, he's torn. He had intended merely to amuse himself with this country girl but love got out of hand, and now he's looking at Giselle, kissing a woman he's supposed to marry, and this isn't the way it was meant to happen. She wasn't supposed to be hurt. But he's a duke. Marrying the daughter of a prince is the direction his life is meant to take, and he can't tell Giselle he's sorry because that would be so insufficient. But she's young, she'll fall in love again, and he is sorry but now Bathilde is not just kissing him, she's demanding that he give her his undivided attention. He tries to steer her away from the eyes of the crowd but the eyes, like spotlights, seem to follow him. And Giselle, in her own spotlight, can see that he's made his choice, not that it ever was an actual choice, he was always going to be with Bathilde, that's the way the world works, and this is when Giselle feels, in the center of her chest, right behind the sternum, not where her physical heart is but where her emotional heart is, a breaking. She can feel it, not breaking like an object might break but turning molten, becoming heavy and black and it's rotting in her chest, exploding and imploding at the same time. And for her, and for anyone, the pain of that is terrible, and it's impossible to run away from your own heart but that's what she starts to do, running in circles at first, running between the cottages to the place where the village trash is thrown away and she lifts a trash can lid. Without looking at the garbage inside she steps in, her toes pointed, one leg then the other and then, still holding the trash can lid, she lowers her body and then covers the can with the lid. And there's silence. The entire village and the wedding party, and Hilarion and Albrecht, they all stare, unspeaking, waiting to see if . . . they don't know what to expect. By now she's already gone mad. If you would try to talk with her she wouldn't understand you. She's lost her reason, literally, her reason for living, and when she does finally pop out, her face is a blank. She steps out, her dress soiled, and with every eye riveted to her she walks to where Hilarion left the sword. It's on the hard-packed dirt, and the reason Albrecht and Hilarion don't go to her and comfort her is because who she is has become another person. And because it's a person they don't know anymore they only stare. Giselle's mother goes to her but Giselle has already begun the transformation, and Pavlova could do it night after night but Giselle doesn't want to be who she is for another second. In some versions of the story what kills her is her broken heart, but in most versions it's the sword, a long, thick sword that she positions diagonally in the dirt, the shiny metal pointing at her chest, and when she drops the weight of her body the point sinks in just below the rib cage. In the Nureyev version, even after he pulls out the sword, as if she's unaware of her wound, she keeps dancing, her hair like her mind, unraveling, spinning around in tighter and tighter circles until finally she falls and there's blood and people rush to her but now she's dead.

In Romantic ballet the tragedy that happens is less about the people than the emotions inside those people. It's not Giselle or

Albrecht who has a tragic flaw, it's love. Inside the crystalline purity of love there's a crack, and as the story unfolds the crack is revealed, and the Romantic part isn't the romance, it's the attempt to stop the crack or hide the crack or glue it back together. Or believe that's even possible. *Rigoletto*, which premiered ten years after *Giselle*, is about a human being trying to hold the world together. Like the dwarves Velázquez painted, he's flawed, and like them he knows it, and like them the emotions he feels are the ones that everyone feels, that I feel, and part of being a father is making sure the flaws of the father aren't passed on to your children. The fact that your blood was running in her veins makes it seem as if you knew her, what her thoughts were, and the games she wanted to act out with you, that you did act out, and I overheard a man in an ice cream parlor stating that all daughters love their fathers. Which first of all isn't true, but it's partly true because daughters learn about men from the first man they know. And changing diapers is part of it but showing her how to live by example, that gets complicated. You grow up with this person, a blind child, helpless and needing you, and you go through the stuffed dogs and the blue bicycles and the need you thought was her need, for you, gets turned around and you find yourself needing her. When Rigoletto, in the opera, finds his daughter's dress on her bed he knows what's happened. His daughter, wanting to escape his protection, didn't tell him about the student she'd been flirting with, is possibly in love with, whatever love is, but because she's not very good at dissimulation Rigoletto suspects some Casanova character has come along, a man like his boss, and it is his boss, disguised as the student, who visits the girl and professes his love. And the same sexist society existed in Rigoletto's time. Knowing her innocence he knows that when she falls in love she'll probably fall hard, and every parent of a girl must worry like this but now it's too late. The girl has already been ravished, and the ravishing is bad enough but now she's in love with the man who did the ravishing. And a hunchback can run when he has to. Rigoletto runs to the stable where his daughter has gone to meet her lover, and at this point he's already hired an assassin to murder the lover, and when he's presented with a body-bag sack he's told it's the man inside, and *a buffoon is a monarch in revenge*. I think that's a line from *Rigoletto*. It's in an aria he sings and then, in the silence after his singing he hears another song, and at first it seems like any familiar song but it's not the song, it's the voice, which can't be right because the man is dead. And if he's not dead, then the body in the sack, the sack at his feet, and at first he doesn't realize what happened, that his daughter, having disguised herself, came to the stable and the assassin, not seeing through her disguise, standing behind a wooden post because that was his job, plunged the knife blade into her back, into the vertebrae, severing the spinal nerves, and Rigoletto, holding the sack, doesn't want to open the sack because he fears what might be inside the sack, but he does. And his madness has already begun. When he pulls at the canvas opening we can't see what he sees, but we see his face, turning numb, the blood flowing out of his face and pooling in his heart. And a young person's heart is still pliable, but when you get old your heart gets brittle, and it takes about two seconds. Whether she's alive or not, like Shakespeare's old Lear, he hardly notices.

When I said before that I wanted my life to be like a dance I meant it, of course, metaphorically. You can dance sitting down. Or weaving between pedestrians on the street. Sometimes I like to get in my car and just drive, more or less mindlessly, without destination, going straight if the light is green, turning if the light is red, following the dictates of the world as manifested by the signals of the world, stopping at stop signs faded by the sun, and the road I'm on now, metaphorically, is the same road I've always been on. The world is visible outside the windshield, and I hear that world humming against my tires, and when I grip the plastic undulations of the steering wheel, I can feel the world out there but without feeling. Just numbness. And there's something seductive about numbness. No pain, no sadness, no disappointment. Just keep holding the steering wheel. There's a crack in my black plastic dashboard, like a rut, and I'm in a rut, and I've made it my rut and I would gladly try something that isn't my rut but the place I end up today is the cemetery. My mother is buried here, on a hill. I park my car, walk down the hill and her stone is here, her ashes beneath it, near a narrow concrete path. It's a flat stone, with her name, the dates of her birth and death, and next to her is her brother, who I never met, he died young, and next to him is my grandmother, who I loved, and then my mother's father, who I didn't know, and there are two ways you can love your mother. The obvious way is to feel nurtured and protected. The infantile feeling of helplessness, like an invisible umbilical attachment, stretches between your two hearts for as long as you live. The other way is the way of understanding. That's how I want to be loved, and it's how I want to love my mother. By understanding the circumstances of her life, born into poverty and hating that poverty, needing to rise above the neglect she might have felt. And of course I don't know what she felt exactly but I know she always seemed to want from me, and from everyone, a sense of both who she was and that who she was had value. And I understand that her need probably altered her love for me, or filtered it, but it didn't erase it. I felt it. I still do. Dead she is but I'm still bound to her, and of course if she would have found the things she craved, one of which was money, then there would've been some extra when she died. I wouldn't have been in quite the same position vis-à-vis Seymour and the Commodore. But that was then and now I'm standing under the cemetery's blue sky, the uneven gravestones pushed up by the earth, or sinking into the earth, and although the earth isn't a fluid, under the crust it is fluid, and it's that thin crust we live on, and we die, and that's why I'm here, to check on my grave. When my mother bought her plot she also bought a plot for me, but the undertakers somehow misplaced my plot or sold my plot to someone else, and the cemetery man said he'd fit me in and now I see they've moved my mother's stone closer to her brother, creating a space for me between her and the concrete pathway. The entire hill is filled with these same stones, the people beneath them with different names and dates, and I wouldn't mind if my ashes were thrown into the open ocean. That's where we scattered my father. But my mother paid for me to be with her, and her name is Freeman, her father's name, probably changed at some point, and names won't matter when I'm dead because, first of all, I won't exist, except in memory, and since memories die when people die it's all the same, the same doing nothing and being nothing, and I suppose at one point I wanted to *be* more, or *do* more, to make my mark as they say. I liked the idea of making my mark. I'd read about people, or heard about them, who made their mark, and that seemed to be what people were supposed to do. When they grew up. Not just supposed to do, wanted to do. When you're young you think you'll do something amazing, and then when you do it, before you know what it is, it's gone, and that's where I am, at the point where I haven't forgotten my dreams but my dreams aren't mine anymore.

I grew up in the house my father built, and although I have no memory of it—we left when I was six—I can see it very clearly, the way he built the walls of the house, with bricks, letting the mortar that held the bricks seep out from between them. Weeping mortar was my father's specialty. Instead of smoothing the wet cement with a trowel, he let it ooze out and harden, like volcano lava hardening halfway over a cliff.

In *Giselle*, the lights come up on a graveyard in the forest. Hilarion, on his knees, is grieving over the grave of Giselle. It's partly the fact of her death, the loss of a person he loved, the girl he wanted to marry and live with and raise children with, but since he was the one who left the sword in plain sight her death is partly his fault. And I know my father killed people in the war but that was his job, supposedly the right thing to do. For Hilarion, to be responsible for killing the girl he loves, or loved, is too much sadness. The regret he feels is not *like* pain, it is pain. And when he walks off into another part of the cemetery he's not softly berating himself, he's doing it loudly, cursing his stupid self in the once-empty cemetery and that's when the Wilis appear. They're led by their queen, Myrtha, wearing a wild headdress, and they swoop down like birds of prey, all in white, a flock of once-beautiful maidens, and they're still beautiful but now their curse is to rise from their graves at night, seeking revenge on the world of men by dancing individual men to death. The specific man doesn't matter, their hatred, born of sadness, is

universal. And even before Hilarion sees them he has a premo-
nition, a sensation we now call the willies, and the word is based
on these creatures, ethereal and dangerous and he sees the Wilis
just before they attack. They surround him, calling to him, and
whether he felt like dancing before doesn't matter because now
he has to dance. It's the power they have. And while he's dancing
he's also trying to resist, trying to pull himself away from what
seems like a magnetic grip, and in fact he is able to pull himself
free, and he runs away into the forest.

The way Myrtha sees it, the women she commands have been
wronged. They aren't evil. And they're not subservient objects
either, or passive ideals of beauty. They're agents of justice em-
powered by anger, and that's what revenge is, a melding of righ-
teousness and anger. They're equal to anyone. And the problem
is, their anger has no resolution. Like insatiable animals, they
feed on death to satisfy a need but the need, which is their reason
for being, can never be satisfied. Myrtha, with her broad, strong
shoulders, knows the story of Albrecht's falseness, and I almost
said manly shoulders but I've only seen her played by a woman,
and when Albrecht approaches the clearing the queen turns to
her new recruit, Giselle. She's about to induct Giselle into the
coven of the unrequited when Albrecht, kneeling in front of
her grave site, sees her. She hasn't become a complete Wili yet
but she's changing, he can see that. And does he even know her
anymore? He stands, approaches her, and it's too late to apologize but yes, he does love her, and then Myrtha gives the com-
mand. Make him start dancing. And because it's night, Giselle
can't disobey. And she knows the dancing will kill him, and she
knows the Wilis want her to kill him. But if she loved him once,

where did love go? And if it didn't go, what can she do? She's cursed, not knowing what will happen until, the moment she faces him, rising up on her toes, extending her leg behind her, her arms stretched in front of her, that's when he takes her and lifts her and she knows her love is undiminished. They dance a dance of forgiveness, spinning and jumping and the forgiveness gives way to pleasure, then joy, and the problem is, to break the curse they have to dance all night. And that's when Hilarion appears. He's lost, disoriented, and a pas de deux is a dance for two people, for Albrecht and Giselle, and because Hilarion is alone the Wilis turn on him, chasing him into the forest and making him dance, spinning him and guiding him, dancing him diagonally to a nearby lake, and he knows he's dancing himself into the water, and he can't breathe under the water, and because he can't stop dancing he drowns in the lake.

My wife and I were left, not with each other, but with a hole we couldn't fill for each other. My daughter was four years, one month, nineteen days when she was taken. And I say *taken* because that's what it felt like, like her innocence and joy had been taken from us. But it was also taken from *her*. Everything good she would ever know was gone, because she was gone, and my wife loved her as much as I did. The years we'd spent trying to preserve her innocence, because innocent is how she came to us, pure and trusting, and suddenly, where there was life, and you think it must be something passing, like a passing thought or dream, but the dream is real and you can't take your eyes away for an instant. That's what we said, and at some point my body couldn't take it. The loss, like a disease, invaded my body, eating away at the organs and bones until after weeks of not moving, hardly talking, certainly not comforting each other or embracing each other, one night I was in the kitchen, watching steam rise from a pot of cooking noodles, and I don't remember how but we found ourselves in each other's arms and we stayed like that, swaying and crying, and I was supporting her and she was supporting me and then I couldn't do it anymore. I couldn't stand. My legs couldn't bear my own weight and she had to hold me, holding me up for what seemed like hours, possibly years, and she had her own strength to preserve and after a while I was too much, too heavy a load, and when she let me go she turned, like a dancer turning her body, and she let me slip from her arms and fall, onto the brown sofa we had, more gold than brown, and I didn't stop falling until I was far away.

Albrecht's problem is that he's still alive. Giselle is dead, and the curse on him is that he has to keep dancing. If he can dance through the night his life will be spared, but at this point, having already danced for hours, his will to dance is exhausted. Whether he's alive or dead hardly matters to him. Which is why Giselle forces him to keep dancing. If she can inspire him for a few more hours then the curse on her will also be lifted and finally she'll be freed from rising up every night and reenacting the same story, over and over, and it's an old story, and it's not even hers. It's Myrtha's story. And when Myrtha returns to the graveyard she sees the lovers still dancing the pas de deux, Albrecht still alive, but barely, and faster, she says, go faster. Giselle does most of the dancing because Albrecht has just about left his body, which is what Myrtha wants, death. She directs the Wilis to surround the couple, taunting Giselle to dance him harder, to break him down, and Giselle can't not obey and so she does, and the dancing takes Albrecht to a place beyond exhaustion, to the point when his body starts to shut down. He doesn't shit himself or wet his pants but he begs to be spared. Which only whets Myrtha's appetite. Her anger feeds on his vulnerability, and Giselle, as a way to protect both him and her own belief in love, lifts him, and like a danseur leading a ballerina she leads him as he once led her, supporting and balancing and embracing him in a dance that continues until the night sky gives way to clouds, in the distance, turning pink. Giselle, by choosing love, has broken the curse. As the sun breaks the horizon, and as the Wilis gradually fade into the morning daylight, Albrecht, looking up from a mossy gravestone, sees Giselle, and we all see Giselle, dissolving into herself, returning to her grave to finally rest in peace.

ACT THREE

La Bayadère

*L*a *Bayadère* was first performed in 1877 by the Imperial Ballet of St. Petersburg. According to the calendar in use at the time it premiered on January 23, with choreography by Marius Petipa, a Frenchman who, working in Russia, is most responsible for transforming a stylized dance for men into what we now call classical ballet. The pas de deux we have is based on his pas de deux. The corps de ballet, which had always been kept in the background, because of him was brought into the spotlight. He died in 1910, on either the first of July or the four-teenth, and the reason two separate dates exist is because in Russia, until 1918, they used the Julian calendar. And any calen-dar approximates the time it takes the sun to get from one winter solstice to another. Now we use a different calendar, with a dif-ferent, more accurate measurement, but because the sun moves as we do, in circular and cyclical and sometimes imperfect ways, as the years go by our approximation of its movement will always be just that.

The story begins with a *bayadère* named Nikiya, a professional dancer who's taken a job at the court of the Rajah. She's still new, unsure about counting the steps, and she's rehearsing those steps on what looks like a nightclub stage. She's wearing a sheer,

Scheherazade-style costume, as are the other dancers, some of them helping her by adjusting her attitude, a ballet position in which the bent leg is lifted behind her. After the rehearsal, when the other dancers have left, Nikiya, thinking she's alone, keeps practicing. She's unaware of the nightclub owner, watching her from behind a fluted column, and the two things that happen in Romantic ballet are about to happen. One is eavesdropping. Because characters in ballet can't talk, the way they gather information is to spy on or listen in, and the other thing is the instantaneity with which ballet characters fall in love. The minute the nightclub owner sees Nikiya he desires her. He surprises her, stepping onto the stage and offering to help her career. He's willing to take her under his wing in exchange for a little affection, which means a little dancing, and when she rejects him, although he walks away, he doesn't completely walk away. He knows the reason Nikiya refuses to love him is because she's in love someone else. Solor, the famous warrior. And when Nikiya goes backstage, Solor, accompanied by orchestral trumpets, makes his entrance. He leaps across the nightclub stage in a series of grandes cabrioles, one leg thrust out, beating the air, his other leg and both his arms radiating out from the center of his torso. This move, like any movement in ballet, when danced by an average dancer, can seem like a stunt or an acrobatic routine. I walked out of a performance of *La Bayadère* one time because the dancer had forgotten the reason for dancing, which is life. A dancer like Nureyev, on the other hand, in the films of him dancing the part, because there was so much joy in his body, his dancing seemed like the natural expression of human elation. And when, after a final leap, Solor finishes his dance, Nikiya appears from behind the curtains. It's not clear if she's been watching him, but it's obvious they're in love with each other. And the way they express their love, and pledge their devotion, is by dancing a passionate dance that pulls them together, leaving them, at the end of it, sweating, sitting together on the lip of the stage, drinking water, unaware that the nightclub owner has been spying on them.

Cosmo's club, the Crazy Horse West, was a strip club. Blinking red letters above the entrance announced the fact of LIVE NUDE GIRLS, and it was true, the girls inside were more or less naked. But unlike other go-go clubs in the neighborhood, Cosmo's shows were all scripted, set in exotic locales, and they were given a touch of tragedy by the master of ceremonies, a character called Mr. Sophistication. He was played by Teddy, created by Teddy, and although he wasn't the star of the show he was the nucleus around which the electrons orbited, the electrons being the live nude girls. His costume for the show was a too-small tuxedo coat, usually a top hat, and on his T-shirt there was a bow tie printed at the neck. He had a puffy face and puffy sideburns, and his stomach protruded, as did his bulbous eyes. It was all part of the Mr. Sophistication persona, which was part Teddy and part made up. He drew an elaborate curlicue mustache on his white-painted cheeks, and when he looked in the mirror before a show he probably didn't see a pathetic clown. He probably saw himself as a highly intelligent human being forced to degrade himself for a living, forced to adopt a personality, which is what we all do, look at the world and be what we have to be. And this made his act ambiguous. He wasn't quite Teddy and he wasn't quite Mr. Sophistication, and when I walked into the Crazy Horse they were rehearsing a new

show, the Vienna number. Teddy was perched on his stool, center stage, and Cosmo was sitting at a table in front of the stage,
leading the rehearsal. Rachel, dressed in a Viennese chamber-
maid costume, parted the curtains, and followed by Sherri, another dancer, walked to a mark beneath a red spotlight. And
although Teddy's microphone wasn't turned on, I could hear the
song he started singing. *Falling in love again. Never wanted to.
What was I to do.* It was more speaking the words than singing
them. *Helpless.* And I felt sorry for Teddy, not because he was
fat, or because he was helpless, but he *was* helpless, and then
he stood up. The girls were standing on various pieces of colored tape, letting the lights shine on their skin, and Teddy, holding a cane, was supposed to walk behind them and spank them.
Instead, he pointed with his cane to the lights, which were too
blue for him, or too bright, or not shining on the right spot,
which was him, and that's when Cosmo stood up, walked onto
the stage, took the cane from Teddy's hand and demonstrated
what he wanted to happen. He walked up to Rachel, looked into
her eyes, mumbled something about *mein Fräulein*, and he raised
the cane as if he was going to punish her and then he laughed.
And then Rachel laughed, and he was passing the cane back to
Teddy when he noticed me standing by the bar. He lit another
cigarette, stepped off the stage, and he must've known I was
there to talk about money, and I didn't have to tell him I was
scared because who wouldn't be scared, and maybe he wasn't
scared because he could pay them back. But I had no experience
dealing with men like the men we played cards with. He asked
me if I'd heard from our friends, and I told him about Seymour's
visit, and about my idea of escaping to Mexico and he told me
not to worry. The worst thing to do is panic. His arm was around

my neck. As long as I owed them money I was a resource, and as long as you're a resource they won't hurt you.

In the next scene of *La Bayadère*, the Rajah has summoned Solor to his house. Gamzatti, his daughter, has fallen in love with a portrait of Solor, like a movie star poster hanging in a girl's bedroom. It's a large oil painting, and she dances in front of it, practicing her extension and practicing her flirtation, imagining the portrait coming to life and turning its gaze on her. The Rajah, knowing about his daughter's infatuation, and wanting to make his daughter happy, has chosen Solor to be her husband, and normally this would be an honor, not something you refuse, but Solor has pledged himself to Nikiya, and when he arrives at the royal mansion he arrives in the middle of a party. People surround a table of food, and musicians are there, crossed-legged on a carpet, and dancers, and although he's cordial to Gamzatti, he keeps his distance. It's tricky because she *is* the Rajah's daughter, and his plan is to be honest, get to know the girl and then honestly tell her that he loves someone else, that she's a beautiful girl and she'll find someone else to love, someone better, but when he and Gamzatti, who is officially his fiancée, sit together on the patterned carpet, although he says these things she doesn't really hear them. His love, he says, has already been given. But don't you like me? And telling her he likes her, even as a friend, is a mistake. She wants to dance, and when she pulls him off the rug and they begin to dance he wants to be sure she understands. You do understand? I can't love you because . . . but she doesn't care. If anything, his lack of interest makes her more determined to spark that interest, and the music she has the musicians play is not quite a striptease song but like Albrecht in *Giselle*, who couldn't *not* dance with the Wilis, Solor feels compelled. Very rarely in ballet will a person be asked to dance and not dance, and when she places his hand on her waist, then moves it up to the side of her chest, he can't not feel the heat of her body, his fingers between the undulations of her rib cage, and possibly because he doesn't want to react, when he smells the perfume she's wearing, he does react. He senses how she wants to be held and he pulls her hip against his hip, not thinking about Nikiya until after the dance is over. But by then he's already made his impression. He mingles with the party guests, and although she keeps flirting with him, and she is beautiful, he leaves the party before anything happens.

I was at a party in college. It was a house party outside Santa Cruz, in an old farmhouse with a local band and at one point, with the singer still on break, the band started playing, not warming up but actually starting into a song. I could hear the progression of notes leading up to a moment when someone would start singing, but because the singer wasn't there, and because I seemed to be the only person aware of this, and hearing what sounded like a standard blues progression, I thought maybe I should step up, that I should follow my impulse, take the microphone, lean into the silver mesh that covered the microphone, and I was smart enough, I thought, to make up a blues song lyric. So I did. I stepped up to a space in front of the drummer, head down, listening for the music to indicate my cue, waiting for the moment when the introduction ended and my voice, together with the two guitars, would begin the song, and while I was waiting for that moment to happen the music changed and the song began without me. The singer returned, took the mic off its stand, and the moment was over. And it wasn't that I was going to become a rock star, but I was about to do something I never normally would have done.

The club was deserted. Cosmo and Teddy and Sherri had left, and since I was alone I stepped up onto the stage. I walked up to Teddy's stool, a spotlight shining on the seat of the stool, and when I sat down and looked out, all I could see was the spotlight shining on me. And because it was on me I was thinking that this is when my solo would happen, my soliloquy. And what would that soliloquy be? Or not be? I was facing out into what they call the house, the audience area, and even with my eyes closed I could still see the red lights, green and pulsating, and I heard footsteps upstairs, Rachel's footsteps in the dressing room. The dressing room was private, and normally I didn't go upstairs but I climbed the steep stairway, like a ladder, and when I got to the top, to the plywood floor of the dressing room, I would like to say I felt at ease but Rachel was Cosmo's girlfriend. She was a stripper, and I was aware enough to know that I was attracted to her, and also that what I was attracted to was my idea of who she was, what I saw not just with my eyes but my mind. When I took a seat she started talking to me, about dancing and her practice of dancing, and about her desire to be seen as something other than a desirable object. And although I was trying to do that, it was hard to separate who she was from what she looked like, which was attractive and tall and dark skinned, her shoulders broad, and when she smiled I found myself going back and forth, thinking about her beautiful teeth and then trying to see past that beauty or beyond that beauty or beneath her teeth to what she was. I was sitting in Teddy's chair, knowing that I didn't know Rachel, knowing that a human being is full of contradictions and complications but still, looking at her I wanted to see something more than what I usually saw, which was usually me, or the world colored by me. And they'd told us in massage class, let your eyeballs fall into their sockets, and when I did I started to notice the halo over Rachel's head, the light reflecting off the mirror behind her, illuminating the outline of the back of her head. And I suppose she thought I wasn't listening because she said my name, a name I hated, although *hate* is too strong a word, but my name was not who I wanted to be. It was innocuous and normal and safe and I wanted to be another name, a Derek, or Alex, or Lex would've been better than the name I was, and her eyes were dark so the whites were very white. Hello? she said, and I said, yes, I'm here. And she was also here, or there, sitting at her table, half turned, and a word can't put its finger on who she was, the person in front of me, a person I was trying to see without disguises, hers or mine, and when I was able, now and then, to see her as simply another human being, not only did I see her more clearly, I saw everything around her more clearly. Black curtains covering the windows, cigarette butts on the splintering floor. The world outside my awareness expanded, or my awareness itself expanded, and there were my own two hands, one of them on Teddy's table, next to a jar of white lotion, and could someone look at the mirror in front of me, or could I look, and see someone in there I wanted to be? That was the question. And still is. And when Rachel told me she had to go home I let her walk down the stairs ahead of me, watching her blue jeans and red shirt, and her round head, disappear down the hole in the floor as she stepped down the steep steps and then she disappeared out the back entrance.

Nikiya, the bayadère, is sitting with Solor, the man she loves, at a sidewalk café. She's questioning him about this wedding, his wedding, and she can't quite believe it. How can you marry someone else if you're in love with me? Nikiya knows about the wedding because she's been hired to dance at the ceremony and she wants an explanation. Has all his affection been a lie? How can you even think of marrying someone you . . . She's rich, is that it? He answers her by standing, taking her hand, pulling her out of her chair, and although she's reluctant at first, or feigns reluctance, eventually, as if she's helpless to stop herself, she starts dancing with him, a dance of misunderstanding that gradually, as her distrust starts to fade away, turns into a dance of reconciliation. He spins her around like a top, as if a top had a mind and he's spinning the thoughts out of its mind, and when she seems to be more receptive he sits her down on his lap and he looks into her eyes, watching her pupils expand. He looks into them and tells her he loves her, and he does, and he doesn't say *only* her but Nikiya isn't thinking anymore about what might come between them. They start touching each other, casually at first, caressing the hairs on each other's arms, and then shoulders and faces and then kissing each other. And when I worked at the answering service what I was essentially doing was eavesdropping, getting paid to pass on what I'd heard. And the nightclub owner was eavesdropping too. Or voyeuring, if that's a word. He was sitting inside the café, at a table near the window, watching the two of them, partly aroused and partly jealous. When Solor offers to show Nikiya his house, to have some tea, she knows what that means, and we watch her agree, and then they walk off hand in hand.

Joseph Cornell would be, according to Haskell's definition, a balletomane. But his mania extended beyond ballet. There are stories about his domineering mother, about his infatuations with young girls, about his collection of pornographic magazines, and they're all about the tension between his sexuality and his disavowal of that sexuality. Cornell, apparently, was in his sixties before he actually kissed a girl on her lips, and *disavowal* isn't the right word because, although his sexual desires were furtive, having been thwarted his whole life, by the time he was in his sixties they were becoming overt. He began spending less time with his mother and more time discovering a world he'd previously shied away from. He started out with ads in the local newspaper, requesting the services of a girl, sixteen or older, to help him sort papers and clip photos, and many of the girls who worked for him reported feeling, as he gazed at them, an erotic tinge to his gaze. Some thought it creepy, some thought it sweet. By this time he was already a famous artist, reclusive but famous, and he was introduced to girls and scouted for girls, and if all went well he would invite them to his house. In his diary he noted their coming into, and then leaving, his life. But not all his crushes were fleeting. He was beginning to work up the courage to find the need to almost want to have a relationship. One woman, an artist in her twenties, posed for him in the nude, and what was it like, at sixty, seeing a naked version of what he'd only dreamed about? It was all real, the skin of her stomach where it curved around the hip to her buttock, the tiny follicles swelling if she was cold, his covering her with a scarf and maybe not by accident brushing an arm against the swelling of a breast. One story has him at a photo shoot for a magazine, hidden in the back of the dressing room while the girls changed clothes, someone hearing his muffled moans behind the curtains, and was he masturbating? It's not that hard to reconcile the man who worshipped ballerinas of the past, who idealized the virginal aspect of girls on the street, with a man who wanted to know these girls physically. The intimacy he was looking for was an intimacy with himself, with the part of himself he'd denied but now, as if waking up from a hundred-year sleep, it was making itself more obvious. He met one girl at the Strand, a coffee shop in Manhattan. He'd wandered in, spotted her, a waitress, and by all accounts she wasn't beautiful, but he imagined in her a purity that was fighting with an impure world and at a certain point, when his interest had grown into something like need, he spoke to her. She was clearing off his teacup and he said something innocuous, the tea was delicious, and she could see that he liked her. She was a runaway, attuned to who might mistreat her or treat her well, and Cornell began a series of meetings. He'd go to the coffee shop, watch her work, make notations in the books he was looking at, and she started coming to his table. They talked, not about art because she knew nothing, but about her life, her difficulties and aspirations, and maybe they were fictitious aspirations because she knew that Cornell, if he was as famous as he said, was probably rich. And inspired by her, Cornell made a group of boxes, the Penny Arcade series, with cut-out cherubs, and pennies, and maps of the constellations. He gave her some of the boxes, his garage was filled with them, and she was the one who gave him the kiss he wrote about in his diary. To her, the arrangement was probably simple. He got a little affection and she got something she could exchange for money. And although Cornell must have known she was selling the boxes, his infatuation with her was worth it. He was tired of dreaming about sylphs and imaginary angels, and now this girl was giving him a chance to step out of his dream, into what seemed like life, and the problem was, the girl started stealing his boxes. He was advised to press charges, which he did, and the girl was put in jail, and that would have been the end of it except Cornell, who saw her through the filter of what he wanted to see, still adored her. He paid her bail and, although he didn't give her any boxes, he forgave her, because he had to, he loved her. He was loyal, to her and his imaginary version of connection with her, and when she died, murdered in a lover's quarrel, he paid for her burial.

The Sleeping Beauty was my daughter's favorite ballet, and one of the things that makes it great is the way it handles time. The princess Aurora is pricked with a needle, and she would die except for the intercession of a fairy, the Lilac Fairy, and instead of dying she's given the chance to sleep for a hundred years. The music is by Tchaikovsky, the choreography by Petipa, primarily, and in a good production you can see that when Aurora awakes, the world she wakes up to, including the prince who just kissed her, is a different world than the one she'd fallen asleep in. The king and queen and all the courtiers wake up, and they dance what seems like an old-fashioned dance, as if the sets and costumes and even their attitudes were from another time. And it doesn't matter if it's a hundred years or a hundred seconds. I remember being with my wife, and naturally, when we slept together we slept on the same bed. Same bed but opposite sides. She had a digital clock on her bedside table and I had one on the table on my side. Often, in what is called the middle of the night, I would wake up, and I would look up at the clock on my side, and it was usually around three or four in the very early morning. If the time on my clock read 4:00, I assumed it was four o'clock. But when I looked over at her clock the time was slightly different. It was either 4:04 or 4:05, depending on when the numbers turned, and the difference was slight in terms of time but in terms of what I was feeling, the emotional difference between me and the person lying next to me, my so-called partner, and she was a partner, not in crime but in history, and the history had failed and now it couldn't go on. Her green numbers said one thing, and mine were red, they said something else, or hers were red and mine were green but it was only four minutes, or five, but that was all the time we needed. It was time enough to wedge us apart, or we did it ourselves, but it doesn't have to end badly. I like to watch the ballerina who plays Aurora at the moment the prince, guided by the Lilac Fairy, kisses her. First a finger moves, then the hand, then the arm lifts, the eyes flutter, and when she comes to life it's a new life.

Cornell lived in a time when ballerinas were part of daily life. It was an imagined time and, for Cornell, an enchanted time, and by all accounts, even as he got older, he was charming. The fact that he was older than the girls he dreamed of might have mattered to someone else but it didn't matter to him. Or more likely, it did matter to him, which is why he sought out younger girls, why Balanchine sought out younger girls, and why ballets portray girls who, like Aurora in *Sleeping Beauty*, are only sixteen years old. In the days of the fables from which the ballets are derived this was a suitable age, a nubile age, but that nubility only makes sense for a seventy-year-old man if the calendar he's using is different than the calendar used by the rest of the world.

Mikhail Baryshnikov was young, only twenty-one when he won a gold medal in Russia for dancing the part of Solor. I mention it because Solor is also young, also a bachelor, and now he's on a date with Gamzatti. They're supposed to be getting married so they're trying to get to know each other, or she's trying, getting *him* to know *her* and be attracted to her, and she's wearing her Salomé outfit, a silk one with jewels. They're in a club, a dance club with a parquet floor, and when the band starts playing she dances for him, her transparent pants meant to tempt him, and they do. She knows what she has to do because she knows about Nikiya, and because she's not quite as beautiful as Nikiya she does everything she can to arouse Solor's affection, to turn it toward her. She's studied the battles he's fought and talks to him about weaponry and artillery, and he finds himself enjoying her company. And marrying a rajah's daughter would be a step up for him. And although images of Nikiya appear in his mind they're just images, and images can trigger excitement but he doesn't need images because Gamzatti, a real person, is right in front of him, pulling him to the dance floor. The musicians adjust their music for this couple who, obviously in love, dance like lovers, her head on his chest, and it's not the kind of dance they dance in ballet. They're not thinking about their grandes sissonnes or how many fouettés they can execute. And oddly, or not oddly, they're not thinking about each other. The needs they have exist independently, and she's getting what she needs, affectionate attention, and he's getting what he must need, confusion. He can't deny an attraction to her, but that attraction is battling with his sense of morality, morality meaning not what's right at this moment but what might be right if he looked at his life from a distance. From a very great distance he would see that he can't get married to Gamzatti. He loves Nikiya. But he does nothing to see his life from that distance, and does nothing to alter the course of where his life is going.

Originally there had been just one Crazy Horse, named after the Indian chief who fought at the Little Big Horn. Then a divorce happened and the Crazy Horse got divided into East and West. Cosmo got the West and the original Crazy Horse burned down and now there was just the one. Down the street from the Whiskey A-Go-Go. It was a Tuesday, and I was driving down Sunset, past the prostitutes and neon signs, able to keep my money worries, at least temporarily, out of my mind, and this is Los Angeles, I thought. The sky was blue and I found a parking spot on the hill above the Crazy Horse. Cosmo was usually there around lunchtime, going over the books or stocking the liquor, but because it was a little before lunchtime I stopped at a nearby coffee shop with outdoor tables. The breeze was warm, the palm trees swayed slightly, cigarette smoke wafted like waves, curling up through the currents of air and my waitress had already brought my coffee. I'd seen her before, and seeing her now, standing behind a chair, a red skirt, a white blouse, a pot of coffee in one hand, steam rising out of it, a used ashtray in the other, I realized that the natural world was everywhere. She was part of it, and the fake flowers on the table were part of it, and I was, and I wouldn't have minded being a bigger part because, nice as it is to look at a flower, I didn't necessarily want to live and die getting my pleasure by watching a brown stalk with petals on the end.

I wasn't ambitious, I didn't want to be famous, although once I did. Stupidly. Los Angeles has more than the usual number of acting schools, and I had no idea what I was doing, this was before the massage classes, and at the time it made sense to take an acting class. Which I flunked. Or at least I wasn't promoted to the next level, kind of an insult since everyone was promoted. But I didn't have the goods. Which is funny. They told me my acting wasn't real. And of course it wasn't real. It's acting. But I was hurt, not so much by them as by my wanting, even when they kicked me out, their approval. And the waitress at this coffee shop was probably an actor, or actress, or wanting to be one, or a model, and I'm not sure why it made me sad, her ambition or my *failed* ambition, but I left a big tip under my coffee saucer. I walked down the sidewalk to the Crazy Horse, stepped up the few steps from the sidewalk, knocked on the door, waited a while then turned the handle. I stepped into the half-dark room, yelling in to the darker part, Cosmo? I walked in slowly, letting my eyes adjust, not so much to the darkness as the redness. I made my way between tables and the chairs on top of tables, and by the time I got to the bar I could see the outline of the room, illuminated by the red glow illuminating the stage.

Cosmo, I assumed, was upstairs in the dressing room so I listened. There were no sounds coming from upstairs, and no sounds coming from behind the stage, and while I was debating with myself whether I should wait for him or try to find him, that's when Rachel appeared. She parted the backstage curtain, walked to the edge of the stage, moving in my direction, pausing at what they call the lip of the stage and then stepped off the lip. Hi, she said. She was wearing a dark raincoat, black or blue, and I as-

sumed she had a leotard beneath it. Cosmo's not here, she told
me. He stepped out. I'm practicing. And then she said, *Vant* a
drink? She said it like Marlene Dietrich, and before I could tell
her I didn't want a drink she told me about the show, giving me a
synopsis that was meant to clarify in her own mind what part she
played in the show. Mr. Sophistication, she told me, has been invited to Vienna by a friend, a long-lost friend, and since he's new
to Vienna, one by one the girls, and she referred to herself as a
girl, offer help in finding his friend. I'm supposed to take him up
in the Ferris wheel, she said, show him the real Vienna, and when
she enunciated *real Vienna* she arched her back in a way that suggested the multiple meanings of what she was saying. But I don't
know, she said, if I should—and she twirled in front of me—
or if I should just say, here's the real Vienna, and open my coat.
And that's when she opened her coat, for a split second, and the
costume she was wearing beneath it was nothing. To help me
find my character, she said, would you be willing to watch me?
It would be a big help, she said. To give her some pointers. And
sure, of course, and so she stepped the few steps between us and
took my hand. She led me to a table where, taking the chair off
the top of the table she told me to sit. Since I'd never actually told
her I didn't want a drink, she brought me one, a glass with ice
and a bottle of scotch, which was Cosmo's drink, and she poured
some whiskey into the glass. A pack of cigarettes was on the table
to my right, Cosmo's brand, and she was grateful, I think, that
someone was willing to watch her, and possibly critique her, and
she was excited when she ran backstage to turn on the music. I
was watching the stage, empty except for the red lights lighting it,
and then the music began rising in volume. The bartender made
tapes for the shows, and this particular music was familiar but

unknown to me, Kurt Weill or Neil Young. It was piano music. And since I was trying not to smoke I pushed the cigarette pack to the far side of the table, crossed my legs, leaned back, and the stage was empty, like a blank canvas, and it stayed blank for a while, which I liked, the idea of possibility, that anything could happen, but when nothing did happen I called out. Are you all right back there? The stage was raised about a foot off the floor, and there was no answer. I didn't know if this was part of the show or if I ought to do something. And if so, what? My plan was to watch her dance, see if there was room for improvement, and if there was, tell her. But now, because *she* hadn't started, my plan couldn't start, and instead of enjoying the suspense of what might happen, I did what I usually did, feel annoyed not at her but at me. And the muscles tightening along the side of my neck, while I waited for her to appear from behind the curtain, or say something from behind it, got me thinking about the twenty-three thousand dollars. The amount of it wasn't as much a problem as the fact that they wanted it now, or soon, and the red lights that lit the stage seemed to alter my perception, both of time and dimensionality. Although the table on my right seemed far away, the stage seemed closer than it was, and when I reached for the scotch and she stepped onto the stage my mind, which had been drifting, came into focus. The twenty-three thousand dollars was just a passing piece of ephemera, a passing piece of something out there, out in the world, out in the world outside the club and I didn't know what time it was out there, or if it was even daylight anymore, and what does she have in mind?

I'd forgotten to puff on the cigarette burning in my fingers, and when she stepped into the light she was wearing the same dark coat but under it, on her legs, she had on harem pants, black and sheer. In the show she wore a matching vest under her coat but she covered herself with the coat, holding it closed, her hands near her neck, and she was trying to dance. I say *trying* because she probably felt awkward, knowing me, and she was trying to warm up to the awkwardness, to work past the awkwardness. And it was funny, and she knew it, and she laughed. Instead of dancing a striptease, which was what I assumed she'd be doing, she began prancing, like a Martha Graham ballerina, running back and forth across the stage, leaping sometimes, her head thrown back, her arms outstretched, and she did some ballet moves, some pirouettes and leg extensions, and the technique dancers use when they spin is to spot the wall, that's what they call it, spotting some object and focusing on that object so that their spinning won't make them dizzy. Rachel was doing that, and also kicking and jumping and more running, back and forth, or maybe it's Isadora Duncan. As she moved across the stage the material of her coat was trailing behind her, like a heavy scarf, and once I got over the fact that she wasn't doing a striptease show, that she was doing something else, a dance show, a balletic modern dance performance, I began enjoying it. I told her, it's great, thinking she might need some encouragement, but she wasn't listening to me. Her eyes were open but she was in her own world, enjoying that world and exploring that world, and I let her continue exploring until, at a certain point, when the music changed, the dance slowed down. The movement became more languid and then she faced me, droplets of sweat on her forehead, her hands above her head, the coat slightly open, and she let her hands slowly fall, her fingers pretending to be like rain, and as she did this she wiggled her shoulders and the coat fell off her body, onto the stage. Then she walked, her feet like the feet of a cat, gripping the floor as she stepped off the stage and walked toward me. I'd started to think she'd forgotten her lines or forgotten what the choreography was, but now, as she stepped onto the carpeted floor of the club she knew exactly what she was doing. Part of being a stripper is being sexy, and she knew that naked-ness is irrelevant. A naked person is only sexy in proportion to the amount of desire they inspire, and for desire to exist there needs to be a connection, visual or physical or mostly imag-ined, and she had her eyes locked on mine, and I must have had mine locked on hers to know that hers were locked on me, and she wasn't Cosmo's girlfriend anymore. I wasn't thinking about Cosmo now, or I was thinking about him less and less as she walked to me, like a ferry boat moving closer to the dock, and as she moved into the dock I uncrossed my legs. I sat up, feel-ing my blood, not the flowing but the pulsing of it, and my re-lationship with Rachel had been based on friendship but here she was, the moles on her neck visible to me, and I don't know what she was seeing but I sat in the chair, stuck like a man who's stuck in a chair, assuming it was a role she was playing because everyone plays a role, and I was expecting to play the role I always played but now she was giving me this other, dif-ferent role, a role I didn't know how to play, didn't ask to play, but I wanted to play, and that's when the front door opened. I didn't notice myself turning back and looking, but I did, and when I did I saw the white daylight past the door, and I saw Cosmo's body silhouetted against the daylight. His walk was distinctive, like gliding, and he glided into the room, past the end of the bar, and I didn't know what he could see because his eyes were probably adjusting to the red light, but they must have adjusted quickly because he walked between the upside-down chairs on tables and he was saying something but I'm not sure what, or to who, or whom, and Rachel hadn't moved, or was just beginning to move, to get up off her knees and she wasn't speaking but I was speaking. I was telling Cosmo to calm down because I could see he was excited. And because he was, his words were unclear, and he was yelling them, and we've done nothing, I said. We're rehearsing. She's rehearsing. It's her job, I said, to practice her part, to get better, and Cosmo walked up to Rachel, and I'd seen his temper, and knowing his temper I grabbed his arm, and I was holding his upraised arms but my grip, it wasn't strong enough or secure enough and I couldn't completely stop him from slapping his girlfriend on the head. And whatever Rachel was thinking, she grabbed her coat, ran across the stage and then backstage and then up the stairs and I said to Cosmo, what's the matter with you? And then he started slapping me, slapping and kicking, and it was halfhearted but it was full of intensity. He didn't want to hurt me but these were his feelings, and they were real, and I was trying to hold his arm but he was muscular for a guy who smoked and drank and we tussled like that, more wrestling than fighting until eventually we lost our balance and fell together onto the once-blue, now filthy carpeted floor. His breathing was hard, his mouth clenched like a fist, and that's when I reached up to the table, to the bottle of whiskey, and to calm him down I tried to lodge the mouth of the bottle near enough to his mouth to pour the liquor down his throat. I don't remember if I told him to open his mouth but I poured as much as I could, over his lips and teeth and most of it spilled across his cheek and into his eye and the front door slammed shut as Rachel ran out, the silhouette of her black coat, and the music, whatever it was, was still playing.

Eavesdropping, as I've said, is a narrative device in ballet. Gamzatti is eavesdropping when the nightclub owner tells her father that Solor and Nikiya are in love. She hears her father decide to kill Nikiya. And because she's not a bad person, she summons Nikiya to the palace dressing rooms in an attempt to bribe her into giving up her boyfriend. Nikiya, naturally, is suspicious of this girl who thinks her wealth can buy her anything she wants, and any person she wants, but Gamzatti is friendly, like a salesman, and as they talk they begin to realize they have more in common than a love of Solor. They like the same clothes, go to the same dancing school, and as Nikiya gets to know her new friend she begins to like her, and when she's given a dazzling gold necklace it's not clear what it means. Is it supposed to be a bribe? Gamzatti doesn't tell her to lay off Solor, but that's the subtext, and Nikiya doesn't like being told what to do. She has no intention of sharing Solor's love, doesn't want half a love, and eventually their discussion comes down to who's going to get Solor. And watching the ballet, I see these two women as two parts of one person, wanting something but getting in the way of oneself, and because the two women are adamant, the conversation comes to an impasse, then turns into an argument, and the argument turns into a fight in which Nikiya, in a fit of rage, picks up a letter opener, which looks like a dagger, and she lifts it, approaching Gamzatti as if she might hurt her. She doesn't know if she will or won't, and that's when Gamzatti's maid comes into the room, and Nikiya, as if waking up, sees what she was about to do and runs off.

The Red Shoes is a movie made by Michael Powell and Emeric Pressburger. It's the story of a ballet impresario and a ballerina, a fictionalized portrait of Sergei Diaghilev and a young girl who becomes his star. The actual Diaghilev brought ballet into the twentieth century with the Ballets Russes, which he founded in 1909. Pavlova danced for him and Coco Chanel designed for him and Balanchine choreographed for him. Originally the movie was to be about Vaslav Nijinsky, the famous dancer who, like the girl in *The Red Shoes*, became the lover of the man who let him dance. In the movie, the ballerina, played by Moira Shearer, a real ballerina, doesn't have sex with the impresario, but when she falls in love with someone else, Diaghilev, or the man who represents Diaghilev, can't stand it. And we don't know the sex lives of Nijinsky and Diaghilev, but they stayed together all those years because Diaghilev gave Nijinsky a way to think about dance. And think *with* dance. Nijinsky's intelligence was not a typical intelligence. His mind, literally, was embedded in his muscles, which is why the ballets he choreographed for Diaghilev, *The Afternoon of a Faun*, and *The Rite of Spring*, were unlike any ballets anyone had ever seen. And because Diaghilev had the talented and attractive protégé he needed, the relationship lasted. It lasted until, on a tour to South America, Nijinsky met a woman, a twenty-two-year-old heiress who, like the girl with the movie posters in her bedroom, had decided that she would become Nijinsky's wife. And did. And whatever his sexuality was, it was fluid enough to allow him to marry her and give her a child, a daughter, and Diaghilev, who heard the news via telegram, was too powerful to be heartbroken, but he was. He fired Nijinsky, who stopped performing with the company, and although he tried, like Pavlova, to perform on his own, gradually, because of war and family entanglements, and it was probably genetic. Nijinsky went mad. Or rather the madness that was in him, that had been released when he danced, having nowhere to go, ate away at his sanity. Asylums were tried and cures were prescribed but in the end his madness became inevitable, and he died in a clinic in London.

At the betrothal celebrations Nikiya's job is to perform and she does her job, but dolefully. She can't help wishing that some event, an earthquake or fire, will stop the proceedings and Solor, holding hands with this other woman, will realize the mistake he's making, and realize who really loves him. And Solor is watching her. He's in the position of wanting her but also wanting Gamzatti, wanting everything he wants and not believing or not realizing or not acknowledging that someone is going to get hurt, and it's going to be Nikiya but what can he do. He's on a path, a path not picked by him because if he picked the path he would be able to love both women. He does love both women, and he still believes that somehow it might still be possible to be with both of them. And while he's thinking this, in the wings, either Gamzatti's maid or Gamzatti's father conceals a snake in a basket of flowers. Nikiya's big solo is filled with battements and grand arabesques, and because she sees Solor watching her, like Margot Fonteyn when she danced the part, aware that Nureyev was watching her, she fills her dancing with longing and passion and when the dance is over people throw roses and money and she's given the basket of flowers. When the old maid tells her the flowers are from Solor she can't help dancing an encore, an encore expressing the realization of a dream. She looks at Solor, then looks at the flowers, and Haskell reminds us that *the face is as much a part of the dancer's instrument as the feet and arms*, and her face is dancing when, looking down to smell the flowers, the serpent rears its head. There's a brief moment of stillness, and then there's a long moment in which, no longer on point, she holds the snake at bay, almost embracing it, grabbing its body as the body slithers out of her hands and eventually the snake sinks its teeth into her neck. She swoons, falls to the floor, and she's not quite dead when the nightclub owner rushes to her side, offering her an antidote. But accepting the antidote means accepting him, and she'd rather die than live without love. And so she dies.

Water under the bridge. That's what Cosmo told me a few days later. He was pouring us each another glass of scotch. We were sitting at a table in the empty Crazy Horse, our glasses on the table, an ashtray filled with dead cigarettes and the whiskey was going down easily. I knew from experience that if it goes down easily at first, it might not be so easy later, but I had to drink. We were having a rapprochement. The incident with Rachel, although nothing had happened, created a tension between us, like a wound, like an injured muscle we couldn't touch because of the pain, but eventually we had to touch it, we were friends, and if we let it heal the wrong way, tight and constricted, our friendship would change, and because we liked the way it was, what we were doing, both of us, was trying to massage the muscle until it loosened, and the whiskey seemed to help because it loosened us. But the wound was tender. Which is why Rachel's name didn't come up. We were both leaning forward on the small square table, our forearms on the table edge, cigarettes hovering above the ashtray, hands hovering above the whiskey glasses, and when he reached over and patted my shoulder it was meant to show affection, no hard feelings, but where was Rachel? He wasn't mentioning her, and I was wondering if he'd fired her, or if she'd quit, but I wasn't asking because Cosmo, like a good magician, was directing my attention elsewhere, to another drink or another laugh. And because no mention of Rachel was made, each laugh became a little less real until, like the famous carriage turning into a pumpkin, I turned into someone who was wishing I was home, in bed, reading a book or sleeping. Only problem, the party can never end because if the party ended . . . I didn't know what would happen, or what Cosmo was afraid might happen, but Rachel was there, between us, not like the haze of smoke encircling us, although that was there, but she was also in our minds. She was in mine when I asked about the Vienna number, how it was coming along, and I knew she was in Cosmo's mind because he didn't answer my question. Instead he took another drink, as I did, and I was doing it for ceremonial reasons. To bond with Cosmo. To mutually forget the person who came between us. And although the drunker we got the more forgetful we were supposed to become, Cosmo couldn't do it. Things happen, he said. And I knew he was talking about Rachel. But what's important. You know what's important? He stood up, and I know he was partly talking about friendship, the bond between men that he must have felt, a cultural thing I didn't feel. And as I say, he didn't bring up Rachel's name and I didn't either, and then he said, Get over here, you. And when I stood up he did what he does when his feelings of affection conflict with his anger. He pretended to punch me. He expressed his feelings physically, and how can men be physical except by hitting each other? He locked his arm around my neck and jabbed at my head, not hard but persistently, and my instinct was to defend myself, which was a way of engaging with him, which is what he craved. And then he hit me a little harder, trying to reach my ribs, to hurt them but also to tickle them. He was using his left hand for punching, his right hand around my head, and when I twisted out of his grip he started slapping at me, using both his hands, still playful, like a dog playfully biting another dog, and although he didn't say put up your dukes, I had to do that, to fend him off, using my arms to parry him but he kept coming, chin down, arms swinging, and the only thing I could really do, and probably what he wanted me to do, was hold him, the way boxers hold their opponents. They grab each other to stop the punching, pulling themselves into what looks like an embrace. And when I did that to Cosmo, he did it back to me, holding me until the intimacy of violence, even feigned violence, turned into its opposite, the intimacy of sorrow, hidden sorrow, and he wasn't mentioning Rachel but there we were, swaying slightly because of the drinks we'd been drinking, not talking, until Cosmo must have felt the moment subside, and when we let go of each other, that's when he said, let's celebrate. He thought sorrow wouldn't catch up to him if he was celebrating, and he took my hand, like a boyfriend taking his girl's hand, and I didn't mention my situation with the Commodore because what was my situation? That I was scared. It wasn't that complicated. And anyway, he couldn't listen to me because he was busy being happy, or trying to be happy, trying to let his bygones leave him alone.

In the movie version of *The Red Shoes*, the Diaghilev character is mounting a new ballet called *The Red Shoes*. It's based on a fairy tale by Hans Christian Andersen. It's about a girl who falls in love with a pair of shoes, a pair of ballet slippers hanging in a window. The shoemaker is something of a sorcerer, and she makes a deal with him in exchange for the shoes, and she wears the shoes to the grand ball and all goes well. And the ballerina character in the movie makes a similar deal with the Diaghilev-like impresario. She can dance as long as she stays devoted to the man who allows her to dance, which is him. And because dancing is what she lives for, she's happy agreeing to that. And all goes well until she meets someone. When she starts falling in love with the ballet's composer, because she's falling in love with something other than him, the Diaghilev character can't stand it. At one point, receiving a telegram in which she asks for her freedom, he walks to the mirror above the fireplace, the crumpled telegram in his fist, and punches the mirror. We see his face reflected in the broken glass, the glass reflecting his broken heart, and he refuses to let her go. He demands that she keep rehearsing, that she not see anyone but him, that she become the girl in the story who, at the end of the evening, is tired. She wants to go home but the red shoes won't let her go home. They aren't tired. The red shoes never get tired. According to Andersen, *They dance her out into the streets. They dance her over the mountains and valleys, through fields and forests, through night and day. Time rushes by. Love rushes by. Life rushes by. But the red shoes dance on.* And at the end of the story the girl dies.

A depressed Solor wanders the empty streets, not quite knowing what happened to him but vaguely aware that he is responsible for causing the death of Nikiya. He's more staggering than dancing, and he staggers into a spotlight in the middle of the empty stage, sits on a carpet next to an opium pipe, and lying on his side like an odalisque, he puts the opium pipe to his mouth. Inhaling the smoke and holding it in his lungs, in his euphoria, he has a vision of Nikiya. She's fogbound, a white figure gamboling in the high Himalayan snow. This is the famous scene in which not only Nikiya, but every member of the extended corps de ballet, flutters down, all dressed in white, and the dance is called the Kingdom of the Shades. These delicate beings are meant to be ghosts, peaceful ghosts unlike the Wilis, and the stage is so crowded with them they're almost amorphous, ebbing and eddying and coalescing around Nikiya. It's a dream so anything can happen, and being Solor's dream, he and Nikiya are drawn together. The music shifts from a languid adagio into an allegro that has him rising, taking her hand, and surrounded by ghosts, he begins partnering her, running with her the way dancers run, in an ever-widening circle, lifting her and sustaining the lift, dancing a dance of reconciliation and understanding. At one point he almost wakes up. But waking up would end the dream, a dream he realizes now he can't live without and so he holds the dream, and holds her, in his mind. And it's a long scene, but it can't be long enough because when it's over she'll be gone, and the music builds to the moment when she makes her final leap into the air, and he catches her, and as he lowers her, his face coming close enough to hers to kiss her lips, that's when he wakes up. Or a squire wakes him up. He's about to get married, and the wedding, when it happens, happens on the steps leading up to the great stone temple. One of the things I remember from school is the names of the old Greek columns. Doric, Ionic, Corinthian. But because ballet is a fantasy, the columns of the temple are crowned with all of them, and with flowers and with statues of elephants. All of it speaks of wealth and grandeur and Solor has come to make his vow, and *vow* comes from *votum*, to vote. Gamzatti is there with her father, and the nightclub owner is there, and Nikiya is dead but Solor, standing beside his fiancée, looking over the crowd of spectators, sees Nikiya. Her tiny, fluttering steps give her the appearance of weightlessness, and she keeps her distance, unseen by the Rajah who's walking his daughter down the aisle, and the nightclub owner doesn't see her but Solor sees nothing else. He's supposed to look at the face of his wife-to-be, into her eyes, to take her hand and vow to her with words he knows but because he can't say them the wedding stops. The music fades and the guests make muffled murmurs. They're waiting, and Solor is waiting, and the ring is in his pocket, and since he's already gone this far he might as well take out the ring and slip it on her finger. But if your excuse is that you've already gone too far, when do you ever stop? Now is the only possible time to stop. But now he's gone too far and he looks, not at Gamzatti but down at his fingers, watching the ring slide over her knuckles, and once he's gone that far it's over. That's when the power Nikiya wished for, the power that is hers in death, finally appears. It comes from above, descending into her and then, like a breath, rising out of her, and whether it's coincidence or whether the power she feels is actually the power of the world, the temple starts to shake. The carved elephants crumble, the thick columns crack and fall, and the guests of the wedding, standing under those columns, are crushed. And killed. Including Solor. And if the theater has the right equipment, although he's dead, he's able to rise from the rubble, join Nikiya, and the two of them, as the lights fade, are borne aloft.

Swan Lake

*S*wan *Lake* is about someone getting older. Prince Siegfried is heir to the kingdom, and when the ballet begins he's having a birthday party, with wine and food and his friends have come to celebrate on the palace lawn. The problem is, he doesn't want to be getting older. He's grown up in a rarefied world of violin lessons and hunting expeditions, and he knows a man his age is supposed to be married, that's what they tell him, or his mother tells him, and he has nothing against marriage, and he likes the companionship of pretty girls, but none of the girls he knows excite him. Some of them used to, but now he's adrift, craving not excitement as much as intensity, a deep emotional bond with another person, and never having found it he's learned to do without it. Benno, his best friend, is drinking more wine than he normally does, enough to provoke him to mention the girl Siegfried used to take fencing classes with, but she's long gone. Another girl, a dancer, was extremely beautiful, but either he was dating someone else, or she was, or he never worked up the nerve to take her in his hand, and now she's gone, and the girls at the party are nice but that's about all. Benno, seeing his friend getting depressed, in an effort to distract him, pretends to be a donkey. He puts on an orange leotard, and when he sticks out his butt he's taunting the others to chase him and catch him, and someone has a fox tail attached to a needle, and that's when Siegfried's mother appears. And when she does the festivities stop. Her face is unsmiling, full of disapproval. She doesn't have to say she finds the levity inappropriate, they know what she thinks, about them and about their influence on her boy, her only child. This is fine for children, she says, but you, she directs a reproach to her son, if you don't get your life in order, my boy, make the changes we expect you to make, that you must *want* to make, then . . . and she gestures a gesture of something like life, some fluid thing trickling through her fingers. Tomorrow, she reminds him, is his formal birthday ball. That's when he will have to act, have to choose the smartest or the prettiest, or whatever he wants, to be his wife. And of course he's agreed to this, how could he not. All his tailors and horses and theater tickets are purchased with her money, making him, in an unspoken way, indebted to her. And worried. He's worried that he won't be able to pay her back, that he won't and can't and shouldn't pretend to love someone he doesn't love, which is what she wants. But he's agreed to try, tomorrow night. That's when he'll face the decision to either obey his mother or obey his heart, and he's afraid he's going to submit to her, resign himself to a world without love, and maybe he's not even capable of love, just good at simulating love, good at giving attention to people, and how can you be so enraptured with another person that you care more for that person than yourself? I felt that way, at moments, with my daughter, but she was my child and Siegfried doesn't have a child. He's the one who's always been a child, and is now, and although part of him questions the romantic notion of perfect monogamy, since he's grown up in a world that promulgates that notion, and since his mother expects her loan to be paid back, there's noth-

ing to say. I'm not looking forward to it, he says, an expression
of muted defiance. Be that as it may, his mother says. And although the full skirt she's wearing is one that, when he was a
child, he used to hide under, now the person wearing the skirt
scares him. Not scares, but he dutifully accedes to her wishes.
And when she leaves the party the guests, who were motionless
when she was there, remain motionless until Benno, in an effort to raise his friend's spirits, suggests a hunt, a great idea, and
everyone starts dancing.

I didn't have a comfortable chair in my house so I was on my
bed, looking at an illustrated anatomy book when I heard the
knock. I had no reason not to open the door, neighbors stopped
by periodically, but when I did it wasn't the neighbors. I hadn't
expected to see the men so soon. I was expecting to spend the
day reading and eating, maybe riding my bike in the afternoon,
but now here they were, Freddie, Seymour, the man who'd dealt
the cards, and the silent crew-cut guy. And the Commodore.
They all deferred to him. He was somewhere in his late fifties,
early sixties, and his teeth were white in a way that didn't look
real. Seymour was the mouthpiece, the one who spoke first. Hiya,
he said, as if we were old chums. He patted my back, stepped
into the house, and as if it was *his* house he invited the rest of
them in. He put his arm around my neck, gave me a friendly
jab in the ribs and they were all acting friendly, too friendly.
The Commodore was whispering to Freddie, who whispered
to Seymour, whose wet saliva was spraying the hairs in my ear
with the same talk at the same time. How you doing? Nice place
you got here. Seymour had already checked out my apartment
and now they were all doing it, sizing it up, eyeing my desk and

the typewriter on my desk, and since they were all talking, to me or about me, I didn't know who to give my answer to, or how to answer, except the Commodore was the boss, I knew that. When he suggested we take a walk, to give us an opportunity, he said, to sort things out, that's what we did. I recommended the Coffee Table, an anonymous café a few blocks away, with sandwiches and pastries, and since it was almost lunchtime maybe they were hungry. I was happy we would be on neutral territory, and as we all walked out of my house, down my steps and down the driveway, I noticed a cloud in the sky. One cloud. And if it weren't for the men I would've stopped, watched the cloud evaporate. But now I was walking with them up the narrow sidewalk, the Commodore and I leading the way, his footsteps longer than mine, mine like a little kid's, trying to match his and catch up, and because we mostly walked in silence, it was a long walk.

I imagine that in the future it will be possible to know about a number of "definitive" Swan Lakes. But I also suspect that artists will want always to change it, to remake it for themselves. George Balanchine said that during his time in New York City. There, with the support of Lincoln Kirstein, he was given a theater in which to restage dance, and remake it, but before he became famous for transforming classical ballet he made up dances in Hollywood, for theater shows and movies. In Monte Carlo, he was Diaghilev's choreographer, and when he was young he danced in Russia, for Petipa. Which is why he called Petipa his spiritual father. And it was during his time in St. Petersburg that he met his first wife, Tamara Geva. She had another name, a Russian name, but like Balanchine, who was born Giorgi Balanchivadze, she'd changed it. He was eighteen and she was fifteen, and after a few years he fell in love with Alexandra Danilova. He went to France with her, and then in Hollywood he met Vera Zorina, another ballerina. He married her in 1938, Maria Tallchief in 1946, and Tanaquil LeClercq in 1952 when she was twenty-three and he was forty-eight. He made them all into the stars of his shows. Ballerinas, he famously said, *are* ballet, and as this succession of girls came into his life he choreographed specific dances for them, each phase of his career corresponding to a different ballerina. And I won't say they were under his spell, but he must have been charming, and his offer to teach them the secrets of dance must have seemed like a dream. And because he was a great choreographer, they were happy to submit to his teaching and his attention, and the relationship worked because all of them got what they wanted. Balanchine got a muse and they got a chance to dance, and to inspire dance, and after a while, after the inspiring quality of each dancer gradually faded, he would find a new dancer. Whether they left him or he left them, the result is the same. The attention you've lived your life for, when that gets taken away, or directed toward someone else, I understand how that feels, and the only thing making it bearable is the thing you've created, and whether it's a child or a beautiful dance, the memory of it exists, and will, and that's the price he agreed to pay. The ballet school had a waiting list, and Allegra Kent was twenty, and Diana Adams was twenty-four, and Suzanne Farrell, also born with a different name, was eighteen when he turned her into a star. He never married her, and probably never had sex with her, but their love affair was mythic. In 1965 he restaged *Don Quixote*, originally choreographed by Petipa, giving himself the part of the leading man, the old Don, opposite

Farrell's Dulcinea. *My interest in* Don Quixote *has always been the hero's finding something to live for and sacrifice and serve. Every man wants an inspiration. For the Don, it was Dulcinea. I myself think that the same is true in life, that everything a man does he does for his ideal woman.* Balanchine was sixty-one at the time, with a bad knee, an incipient heart condition, but he was in love, and the difference in age was irrelevant. Or it should have been. Like Filippo Taglioni teaching his daughter the steps that would make her a legend, it wasn't the steps that mattered as much as the spirit animating the steps. And that spirit doesn't just appear. You have to work to make it appear, to find it and nourish it, and everyone does that in a different way. Taglioni *père* might have been strict with his daughter, holding a stick in his hand as he told her to extend more, to elevate more, to hold her leg in attitude until it hurt. *Some people are hot*, Balanchine said, *some cold. Which is better? I prefer cold.* Either way, Balanchine must have been an amazing teacher, and sometimes a person needs to be shown the cliff and sometimes a person needs to be pushed off, and Farrell probably needed Balanchine as much as he needed her.

The moon is up, nearly full, which is perfect for hunting swans. Benno has seen some near the lake, and now Siegfried is part of an expedition, a swan-hunting expedition. It begins with his friends flushing out the brush leading up to the lake, and Siegfried is the only one without an arrow in his bow. He's not that interested in hunting. Hunting requires a degree of testosterone he just doesn't feel, and he leaves the group. He wanders alone through the undergrowth, stepping over puddles and jumping a stone wall, and he's walking down a fire road, two ruts with grass growing between them, when he sees a flock of swans. He's seen turkeys on the property but these are white, larger than swans but with heads held high on the tops of their necks, and as much as he can he follows them, down a narrow trail to a large pond where the swans are gathering. With his bow in one hand, he reaches behind his back to his quiver of arrows, and under the moonlight, positioning himself behind a rock, he readies the shaft of an arrow and aims his bow. He looks from swan to swan. They're preening in the shallow water, and he sees, in the middle of their choreographed fluttering, one particular swan. Except she's not a swan, she's a woman. She's wearing a feathered shawl, and she's got a feather pinned to her hair but she's human, perfect and beautiful. And he'd drawn the bow but now he lets it slacken. He approaches her, slowly. The other swans, like her, are human, and they disperse when he comes to the edge of the pond. He was hoping not to frighten the one, and unlike the others, when she sees him, she keeps her ground. She covers her breasts in a way that makes her look frightened, so he puts down his bow. He lifts his hands in a gesture of peace and sincerity, signaling her not to go, to please don't go, and he can see the human swan beginning to relax. That's the first step. He's willing to stand there all night to show her, not only that he means no harm but that, and this is one of those sudden times in ballet, he's fallen in love with her. And she must be going through something similar because rather than turning her body away from him, she faces him, exposing the open front of her body. Her head, which had been resting on her shoulder, turns and she holds out her hand, inviting him to what, to dance? Then she wades out of the water, moving her feet through the dark water and her body, from her thighs down, is wet. She's wearing what looks like a white feathered bathing costume. In a clearing by the pond she brushes the water off her arms and legs, and this is the movement that precipitates the dance they dance, a dance of acquaintance and trust, and it starts with their slow circling each other, not touching at first, but that happens, and once they realize they love each other, after their dance, they sit on a smooth rock by the pond and talk. He listens to her story, about a princess named Odette, and about a sorcerer who put a spell on her. At night she can be who she is, a woman, but during daylight hours she's been cursed to take the body of a swan. I say *cursed*, but it's the deal she made with Rothbart, the sorcerer, or sometimes he's called von Rothbart, and either way, when the sun rises, feathers sprout into wings on her back, and all the girls are cursed like that. Swans in the day, and at night they all become women again. Siegfried thinks there must be something he can do to help, and that's when she tells him about the antidote, if curses have antidotes. The sorcerer's spell can be broken, she says, if someone vows to love me forever, and faithfully. And he's about to swear his love when Rothbart appears. He'd been watching them from the trees, and now he steps over some lichen-covered rocks and moves to Odette. He's got a large silver belt buckle and he moves to her in a way that implies ownership, as if you can own someone. She pulls herself away from him and, that's enough, Siegfried tells him. Leave us alone. And Siegfried doesn't feel himself under a spell but even as the words leave his mouth they sound impotent. And he feels impotent. If the sorcerer is actually a sorcerer then there's nothing he can do but stand there, his feet on the damp earth, not quite catatonic but unable to perform the act. That will save Odette. All he has to do is promise his faithfulness, and that's easy, and he's about to do it when Odette reminds him that if, for any reason, he proves unfaithful, then the spell will require that she die. I understand, he says, and even if he doesn't understand, he swears to her that he loves her and will honor her, and then Rothbart laughs. He has a full beard, half red, half gray, and because his laugh is a laugh of derision Siegfried impulsively steps forward, and I know the feeling he has, of wanting to hurt Rothbart, to bash his skull in. And when Odette steps between them, her arms extended, her palms facing each of them, that's when Siegfried ought to forget about Rothbart, turn to Odette, and realize his love is right in front of him.

At the coffee shop no one, apparently, had an appetite. The Commodore sat across from me and although I would've loved a cup of coffee, no one was offering. No one was offering because no one was talking. The ceiling was low and the walls were yellow, and I found myself watching a painting on the wall, of a ship's porthole. A local artist had put up some paintings, and I say *watching* because I could see the sky on the other side of the porthole but I couldn't see below the sky to the ocean. The ocean, if you look at it from outer space, is calm and blue, but if you're on the ocean, or standing on the rocks next to the ocean, it's deadly. And that's what it felt like in this café, the air blowing out of the air conditioner, not like an ocean breeze which is neutral, but like life, and what matters in life is how you deal with the events of life, but there was no decent way to deal with this café. Except to get out. And I couldn't get out because Freddie was sitting next to me. Plus the matter of the twenty-three thousand dollars. That's what I owed these men. I won't call them gangsters, and it doesn't matter what I call them. I didn't have twenty-three thousand dollars, had nowhere to get it, no rich uncle. Cosmo would've been my rich uncle, but once he'd paid his own debt he was broke, or so he let me know. And yes, I was stupid. I'd let myself get carried away. But that was the past. The question now was, what do I do, or what could I possibly do except hope. But hope, I realized, was the stupid thought that got me here, and now I had to move forward. Take one step forward. This is where I am, and what I am is how I live, starting now. It isn't a life I ever wanted or expected or dreamed of, but this is me, and it always looks worse, at the moment, than it will in a week or a month or years from now. When I'm older, I thought, I'll look back on this and ha-ha, what an experience I had. When I owed a group of criminals, who might possibly be murderers, that money. Twenty-three thousand dollars. Unless they're going to forgive my loan. People do that. Twenty-three thousand dollars to them is probably a pittance. Never let this happen again, they'll say, or the Commodore will say it and I'll say, no sir, and he'll tell me to go. Or maybe he'd tell me to do something else. I was like his doll. When Freddie elbowed me on the banquet seat I was like a stuffed animal, and the Commodore's hair was gray, his face tan, and he must have had a skin disease when he was younger. And I didn't speak because I was waiting for someone else to speak. I was still hopeful. Not full of hope, but I had some, and then the Commodore, as if waiting for the hum of the air conditioner to quiet down, when it didn't quiet down, looked up. And I pretty much knew what he was going to say. Pay us or we'll hurt you. That's how they did business. And when he did finally speak there was no preliminary chitchat. You owe us a lot of money, he said, and I said yes, I know. And I'm sorry. I sincerely intend . . . but he cut me off. They'd already taken my credit cards. There wasn't anything else. Whatever you want, I said. I'll pay you back. One time I ate at a restaurant without having money to pay for my meal, in Reno, Nevada, a lavish meal, with steak and wine and when the waiter brought my bill I pleaded ignorance, asked if I could wash the dishes. I'd heard of that being done but it wasn't done at that particular restaurant, and the manager called the police, and only because it was a busy restaurant was I able to escape. But twenty-three thousand dollars. That was serious money, but yes, I said, I can pay it back. No problem. And in my mind there was no problem because this was what I had to deal with, at this moment, and the next thing that happened, I'd deal with that when it happened, and yes, I told the Commodore, and he said, yes what? He sat, his hands on the table, and the other men were either looking at him or looking at me, smiling beneficently, or maybe the word is *benevolently*, and I kept saying yes, affirming the Commodore's words, and affirming their power over me, and affirming my acceptance of the role I'd been given, a role I didn't want but couldn't fight because first of all I was outnumbered, and second, I really did owe them money. And when the other men joined the conversation, asking about my life, about my family and my love life, they seemed especially interested in my experience in Vietnam. You were in the war, right? I wasn't, but yes, I told them I was, and I was surprised how quickly the answer came out of my mouth. Did I see much action? Action? You know, Seymour said, and I knew what the term *action* referred to, combat, and I was about to respond when Seymour elaborated. Ever kill anyone? And yes, I told them, I killed a few people. How can you not? And they understood. Not that I'm not proud of it, and of course not, they said. There was a line they'd drawn, not on the floor but in their minds, clear as chalk, and now I seemed to be crossing the line, from my side to their side, and it was almost friendly again. I was sitting on the bench seat against the wall, Seymour in a chair to my right, Freddie on my left, the crew-cut guy and the dealer at a different table and I was facing the Commodore. I was aware of my so-called sitting bones on the cushion of the bench, my femur bones extending out of my hip sockets, my legs connecting to my feet on the floor, and rising up from the floor I could feel a current of energy, spiraling up into my pelvis, up my ribs and spine and by thinking about the structure of the body I was trying to be relaxed, relaxed and nonchalant. They wanted to know what gun I'd used in 'Nam, the name of the gun, and I nodded as if nodding was an answer. And it must have been a kind of answer because the talk, swirling from the general topic of killing people in war, began to eddy around the specific topic of killing Asian people. It turned out they had an associate, a Chinese guy, not really an associate, they called him a punk at first and then a bookie, a bookie down in Chinatown who was into them for *mucho dinero*. Seymour was doing the talking now, and you can help us, he said. He pulled the hairs of his mustache away from his nose, and as I listened to him I knew, even before he finished, where this was going. I may have been dumb but I wasn't a fool, and looking at Seymour and the Commodore and then Seymour again I said, if you want me to kill this guy for you . . . and I waved my hands in the air as if I was swatting away an insect. Not swatting, but if a bee would come buzzing around my head, instead of antagonizing it, I would steer it away, as gently as possible, to let it know that this is not the time or the place, and I think my gesture was pretty clear but maybe it wasn't. Or maybe it was, but it wasn't the gesture they wanted.

Siegfried can see the sky in the east turning pink, and he knows he doesn't have much time. He wants Odette to stay a girl but he can already see the downy feathers appearing on her neck and shoulders, and at this point Rothbart is gone. A harp is playing in the distance, in B minor, not very loud but it's enough to get the lovers, that's what they are now, to dance. Siegfried gestures with his hand, come join me, and when she takes his hand he leads her in a dance that was probably choreographed by Lev Ivanov. *Swan Lake* had existed as a ballet before 1895 when Petipa, seventy-six years old at the time, remade it for Pierina Legnani, the prima ballerina assoluta of the Imperial Ballet. Although he doesn't get the credit, Ivanov, who was Petipa's assistant, is the one who understood the complexity of Tchaikovsky's music, and the dances he made express the somber mood of the minor key by sometimes subverting it. The interesting part of the dance for me is when Odette starts spinning, when Siegfried cradles her without touching her, his arms forming a circle around her spinning body, letting her spin like a top until like a top she can't spin anymore, balanced on the points of her toes, her arms raised, a vertical line for as long as she can and then when she falls, at the bottom of her fall, he catches her. They do this several times, and what Ivanov shows us is her trust. She's tentative at first because she's testing him, and every time he catches her he's proving his love and the strength of his love, and the trust she feels is liberating. But now the pond and the sky and the mountains surrounding the valley are getting light. She sees the light, or feels it, and says, I have to go. She's under a spell. But Siegfried doesn't believe in spells, he doesn't want her to go, and Balanchine didn't either. When Odette turns to join her sister swans, Siegfried takes her wrist, like Balanchine when Suzanne Farrell decided to marry someone else. He couldn't stand it. He had to stop her. The idea of her leaving him, even for an instant, he couldn't believe it, but because the curse was in front of his eyes Siegfried had to believe it, and they stand like that, their bodies pulling in opposite directions until, because her wrist is wet, he loses his grip, and almost like walking on water, Odette wades back into the mist of the pond and disappears behind some reeds. When Benno, the friend, walks into the glade, Siegfried wants to know if what he saw, the person he saw, the person he held in his arms, but of course she was real.

I knew it before, but sitting with these men, their hands on the table, the hairs growing out of the backs of their hands, I could see their friendliness was only a veneer of friendliness. And the thinness of that veneer became obvious when Freddie, who seemed to be the most volatile, certainly the most emotional, possibly retarded, pounded his large hand on the table. Make him pay, he said, make him pay. He owes us money, he should pay us back. And if they were playing good cop/bad cop, Freddie was the bad cop and the Commodore told him, relax. We're all friends here, he said, and friendship is more valuable than—and he did his own version of swatting away a bothersome insect— financial considerations. That's what he said, but then he said that something had to be done, unfortunately, about the financial discrepancy, the money I owed. He pretended to think about this thing he called a situation, and how it might be turned to everyone's advantage. His hair was like a manicured lawn, damp not from dew but from hair oil or hair tonic, and like gravestones on a cemetery lawn he didn't seem to be moving. He was quiet. And I was quiet too, waiting for the questions, most of which I answered truthfully because the best way to deal with situations like this, in my experience, is to tell the truth. I could have made up a story about coming into money, some investment I'd made. Or I could've pretended I was a wealthy heir apparent waiting for my trust fund. Or that I was insane, a buffoon. I could have started playing a role, and certainly they were playing roles with me, but even when you play a role you have to tell the truth. Within the confines of any role a certain amount of truth is going to leak out, and it should leak out, and the problem was, I didn't know what role I was playing. Or what I wanted to play. I told them about my father. One of his businesses was a dry-cleaning shop, in San Diego, in one of the first shopping malls in the world, or so he told me, before they were called malls, and I didn't go into detail because I didn't know the point of the story. Stalling, that was the point. And by stalling I was revealing what I was, a middle-class kid who'd tried to *be* good, or *do* good, but not really, because what good had I ever done. I wasn't a kid anymore. I was a grown human man, and the past I'd had was over, and I was moving on, not forgetting because I would never forget, and by trying to forget I'd gotten involved in a gambling game, which was stupid to do, I was sorry I did it, but I wasn't the kind of person who could hurt someone. I can't do that. And although I wasn't an adamant person I was adamant about this, and if we wanted to come to an agreement, that was fine, I wanted an agreement too, but it would not involve killing another human being. Those two things are immutable, I said. Off limits.

What two things?

What?

Two things are off limits?

The night of the birthday ball has arrived. Siegfried's mother, who designed the festoons, is proud of her party, and she asks her son if he's happy, meaning happy with the decorations. He, of course, is thinking about Odette, whether she'll come, and when, but he does as his mother instructs him. He sits on the dais while she, tapping a champagne flute with a spoon, gets everyone's attention. This is the moment of his big decision. Six beautiful girls are brought in, girls his mother has chosen, and in a way they're auditioning for him. Each one dances a dance from her part of the kingdom, and Siegfried dutifully dances with each of them. But none of them stir his blood, that's the expression, the way Odette does. It's either blood or a chemical, or an electrical charge in his body. And when the moment comes for him to choose, because he doesn't feel it, he can't choose, and that's when the door opens and a man with a red beard leads his daughter into the hall. Everyone turns, and she's stunning, dressed in black feathers, and at first Siegfried doesn't recognize her. But then he does, her face, but Rothbart has disguised her real face. He's disguised himself, and the daughter is his real daughter, Odile, who's been transformed into a version of Odette. An exact replica. The ballet version of the story has the two roles played by the same ballerina. And Siegfried, thinking he's talking to the girl he loves, when he asks her to dance, he doesn't notice her dancing lacks passion because he's dancing with his dream, and what could be better. He's showing his mother, and the whole world, the person he loves, the proof that he *can* love, which takes his attention away from her. He's not looking into her eyes, which would tell him she's false, and his mother's not looking because she's being charmed by Rothbart. Tchaikovsky's music is perfect for a solo, and after Odile performs it Siegfried joins her and she's almost exactly like Odette. They dance together, spinning and lifting, and Odile becomes confident that her mask is fooling him and she toys with him, running from him, laughing at the power of controlling him. Only Rothbart, from his perch on the dais, sees Odette, standing outside the window, frantically flapping her wings to get her lover's attention. He signals to his daughter who, seeming to be coquettish and playful, covers Siegfried's eyes. And then, standing at the center of the hall, she executes the requisite thirty-two fouettés, a display of technique made famous by Legnani, in Russia, and *fouetté* means *whipped*, and having seen it, and seen her, Siegfried goes to the man with the beard and asks to marry his daughter. Yes, he says, but with one condition. He demands an oath, which Siegfried readily gives. He swears his love for this beautiful person in front of him, proclaiming to the world his desire to make her his wife. And as the music fades and the hum of the party subsides, that's when we hear the knocking on the window. We see Odette, her long neck the neck of a swan, her face pressed to the glass, tears running down her cheeks. She's crying because Siegfried, unwittingly or not, has pledged his love to another woman, and also because, by the law of the spell she's under, now she has to die.

Across the café I noticed a man and a woman sitting at the table. They were looking at a document, a screenplay probably, and above them a fan was turning, the blades of the fan angled in a particular way, and I didn't know if the people felt the breeze of the fan but this was when I realized I was scared. I was sitting at this table, my back against the wall, surrounded by faces that would as easily hate me as love me, more easily probably. And hurt me, and the expression that comes to mind, *out of my depth*, doesn't seem right or descriptive because at that moment I was *in* a depth, deep in a depth, and I might've wished I wasn't but I was, and Seymour said to me, you said two things are off limits. What two things?

Killing someone.

That's one thing.

I wouldn't be able to do it, I said. When I'd let them think before that I'd seen action in Vietnam, that wasn't a complete lie. I had seen action, in a way, but the action I'd seen was on television. I'd been too young. And although I never actually told them I was over there, in the jungle, in combat, by letting them think it, I was lying. And I didn't like lying. A lie is like a fist. It's closed and tight and it can hurt someone. Lying is also like taking a first step, the first step determining where the next step will go and with each step the weight moves forward, creating the momentum that necessitates another step and then another and I wanted to be transparent. I wanted them to see who they were dealing with, an innocent person. A nice guy. Not that I was being completely myself, and not that I knew who I would've been if I had been myself, whatever that was, because, although I wasn't calm, I was trying to seem calm. I was scared of these men, and the fear I was feeling would have been evident if they had looked behind my seemingly calm demeanor. I was trying to act casual, trying to seem as if talking with criminals was run-of-the-mill, as if mills still existed, and murder, which was basically what they were hinting at, was par for the

course, and although it was a course I never played I was nodding with them, almost one of them, or like them, and we were
all in the same boat except the boat I was in had holes in the bottom, and it was sinking, and as they watched the water pooling
up around my feet and my legs the Commodore did his thinking
face again. He put his fingers to his lips, rubbing them across the
dead skin covering his lips and the other guys were waiting for
him. And I was also waiting. In any negotiation you have to ne-
gotiate, even if you have no power whatsoever, from a position of
seeming power, and once I'd made my case there was a stillness
at the table. The sound of silverware, like a hum, or like waves,
not crashing on plates but washing over them, echoed across
the room and then the Commodore cleared his throat. He said
there might be a way to reduce my debt. Not erase it but make
it more manageable. What might be arranged, he said, was for
me to go to Chinatown. Not to kill anyone, don't worry about
that. Just go down there. Take some pretty girls. I'm sure you
have friends, and take these girls because the person we want to
talk to, this associate of ours, he has a weakness for pretty girls.
What I was supposed to do was use these so-called girls, who he
imagined I was acquainted with, to lure this Chinese businessman out of Chinatown. That was it. Do that, and they'd do the
rest. And for my trouble, the Commodore said he'd knock off,
and he pretended to be doing the math in his head, say ten thousand dollars off your debt. And I took some time pretending to
give that some thought, but not too much thought, and although
we didn't shake hands we both agreed we had ourselves a deal.

The stories of the great ballets are mostly unbelievable. There
are no sylphs or Wilis or women who turn into swans. But the

emotions inside the stories, the loss and betrayal and obsession, they're the same ones I've known except now they're happening in a castle ballroom. Odette, who's been watching from outside the window, once the clock strikes midnight, once she's able to assume her human form, runs in to the ballroom. She's been crying, and still is, her face red and swollen, her hair falling into her eyes. She's been deceived, as Siegfried has, but just because a dream deceives us doesn't mean it's wrong. That's what Foucault says, and because Siegfried's dream was a dream of desire, under the spell of Odile, who embodied that desire, he was blinded. And it takes him a while to realize what just happened. It takes a while because, like the muscles in our bodies, our minds, once they get accustomed to a way of believing, keep believing that way, and when she tells him she has to go, that she has to leave him, forever, he can't believe it. He thinks she's worried about that woman, Odile. But I don't love her, he says, I love you. But it's not Odile she's worried about. It's the promise. You made a promise, and now you've broken your promise. And it's true, he did, but that was a trick, what could I do? And it doesn't matter now, he says, because now we have each other, that's what matters. When he looks into her face he hears himself talking, hoping that what he's saying might be true but knowing it's not, and a good dancer, or a dancer who's a good actor, is able to communicate that confusion. Nureyev, when he danced with Margot Fonteyn, was able to feel the hundreds of emotions swirling around in his body, and when confusion, or any of them, rose to the surface he didn't pantomime their appearance. He felt his life being taken away. Margot Fonteyn was nineteen years older than he was, but to him she was still a girl, an innocent young girl, and he'd pledged his life to her and now he's broken that pledge, and like a man being torn in half he can't believe it happened.

As George Balanchine got older his wives got younger, or at least the difference in age between them got greater, which was only natural. Ballerinas came to him, and some of them inspired him, and when he was inspired he couldn't help it, he fell in love. And the term *love*, in this case, sometimes implied sex. We don't know what his intimate life was like but we can imagine that, as old age took its famous toll on him, he wanted to keep his vitality. He made his dances by dancing them, and he wanted to keep making the dances that gave him his reason for living. But how do you hold on to something that's already gone? That was his question. Although it was easy enough to *feel* what a young person feels, how do you *do* what a young person does when the body doesn't want to do it? Maria Tallchief, who was married to him for six years, said their marriage was filled with passion, but it was a passion for dance. And that was fine with his wives, they loved him for that and were satisfied, but he was not completely satisfied. He felt the difference between what he was and what he had been, and in an effort to regain what he had been he attempted some cures. That's what they were called. They usually happened in clinics in Switzerland, and sometimes they involved injections. And it's logical, given the science of endocrinology, to think that hormones taken from one body, even if it's an animal body, even the testicles of sheep for instance, might be used to supplement the hormones in another, human body. Since he was often flying to Europe, it wasn't hard to visit one of these clinics, and I picture him, sitting in a straight-backed but comfortable chair, a yellow chair, and there are plants in the room, it's an expensive clinic. He's not wearing his bolo tie because that's his trademark, and he doesn't want to advertise his presence. He's just a man, an average, regular man in a brightly lit waiting room, and because it's an expensive clinic it's not like a typical waiting room with other people. It's just him, sitting with a coat, a shirt, no tie, and there might be magazines on a table but he's not reading them. His feet are about hip width apart, his knees over his ankles, his hands on his knees, and he probably knows what he's doing isn't healthy. The fountain of youth, by it's nature, is poisonous, but what's his choice? He can grow old, stop dancing, stop being with beautiful ballerinas, or he can try something, and he does, choosing to dance even if it kills him.

Nureyev, dancing for the Kirov Ballet in Russia, was already a star in 1961. He was loved in Europe and loved in Paris and he loved Paris in return. When the Kirov toured the French capital Nureyev took advantage of the freedoms he didn't have back home. This was the beginning of the swinging sixties, of disco balls and pop art and turtlenecks worn unironically. He had minders, KGB guards meant to watch him and keep him in check, but part of his genius, and his greatness, was the impossibility of keeping him in check. He'd been introduced to a socialite, a wealthy, unmarried woman who, along with other dancers and actors, frequented clubs and parties, and I don't know what deal he had with the socialite but the minders had to follow. I don't know if drugs were involved but there was probably drinking, and at this point there was also the question of Nureyev's homosexuality. It sounds old-fashioned to talk about homosexuality as if it's a thing, different than any kind of sexuality, but at the time it was considered questionable, even taboo.

And after the company's engagement in Paris it was decided, by the KGB or the Politburo, that Nureyev was getting too wild, that he was expressing unwanted ideas, that he would need to be taken out of circulation. It was decided to bring him back to Leningrad, and maybe to prison, and because he expressed himself by dancing, and would certainly have to stop dancing, it would probably kill him.

Style. That's the word we use when referring to outward expression. *Style makes the man,* that's what they say, meaning that we don't choose style, style chooses us, making us who we are, which is why I was trying to be stylish. *If you lack a trait, assume it.* And I was trying to assume that I could do the job I'd been given, find this Chinese man, and normally I wouldn't have been concerned with style, but style meant expressing yourself. It's why I'd put a carnation in my lapel. Cosmo wore carnations, but I wasn't doing it because of him. He'd been my guide for a while, and my benefactor, but now I wasn't using a guide, not him anyway, but he offered to do me a favor. He couldn't pay my debts for me but he did arrange for his driver, Lamar, to pick up Sherri and Darlene, dancers who worked in his club, and have them spend the day with me, in Chinatown. That's where we were, driving along the hot streets in an air-conditioned limousine, and this isn't bad, I thought, meaning life, meaning the good life, the enjoyable life, and the trick is slowing it down. The technique of finding happiness involves slowing down, and when happiness appears, even if it's only for a fraction of a second, realizing it. And enjoying it. Which takes work. But if you're willing to do the work, which I was, and the girls were, and Rachel no longer worked for Cosmo. She'd quit I found out, gone back to doing whatever dancing she'd been doing before. But Sherri and Darlene still worked for Cosmo, and I didn't know if he was paying them but when we found a café in what seemed like the center of Chinatown I told Lamar to stop. We were overdressed but that was all right. We wanted to be noticed. We walked into the empty restaurant, empty except for tables, a kitchen in the back, and a silent television by the cash register. When we sat, we didn't put our arms on the table because it was greasy. And the menus were greasy but we ordered food, and I hadn't told them why we here here and I didn't tell them now. I told them, periodically, to check outside to make sure the car was still there, hoping that when they walked outside, in their bright dresses, the bookie we were supposed to be looking for would notice them. Other than that it was just waiting. Waiting, and since there wasn't much talking there was room for thinking, first of all about money. The money I'd lost was a fact. And I was dealing with that fact. The other thought was about being a loser. Although I'd never thought of myself as a loser, that's what I was, and the money I'd lost was peripheral to the fact that I'd lost it, or it would have been peripheral except it wasn't just *my* money, it was the Commodore's money. And the only way to be happy, in the face of the fact of being a loser, is to acknowledge what you are and acknowledge what you've lost, and I can't go back in time because I've lost that too, what I used to be or what I used to think I wanted to be, and now I was something else. I couldn't deny it because it always comes back, the truth, to roost as they say, so I told myself, okay, fine, I'll be a loser. But I would be my own *version* of a loser. And by being my own version I would be comfortable, and by being comfortable I would be able to salvage a certain amount of, not happiness but like Rachel dancing. *Be yourself.* That's the expression she used, and Rachel didn't love stripping but she was good at it because, when she took off her clothes in front of an audience she was comfortable being herself. And she thought being herself was the same as revealing herself but the only way to remove your clothes in front of a bunch of strangers is to create a personality, pretend to be that personality, and from the security of that pretense you can be naked. And that's how she did it, if she thought about it. What I was thinking about was killing someone. The thought was still an abstraction to me because, although everyone I'd truly loved had died, death was still an abstraction. My father and mother and my child had all died, and I'd seen my father and mother when life left their bodies but I hadn't absorbed in myself, or hadn't allowed myself to absorb, the reality of death. I only knew the reality of things I did, eating food and having sex, and riding downhill on a bike with the wind in my face, the road vibrating beneath the tires, and it was because I'd never killed anyone. I'd never fought in Vietnam, and maybe I should have because then the fact of killing wouldn't have been hidden. Which it was. It's why the image of death is hooded, carrying a scythe but unseen, therefore unknown. And although we all know that everything dies, there's a gap between knowing in our minds and understanding in our bodies, and this Chinese man they'd told me about, because he was an abstraction I could say yes, I'm willing to kill him. But I wasn't. Because I knew the event itself wouldn't be abstract. The actual act of ending the life of a person like me, or enough like me, it was impossible. Let *them* kill him if that's what they want. So I thought. But there I was, working for men I found reprehensible, an accomplice, sitting in a bright fluorescent restaurant, more like a café, with Sherri and Darlene, using them as bait to lure this Chinese bookie, like a fisherman, and because no one seemed to be taking the bait I kept waiting for something I didn't want to happen to happen.

The details of Nureyev's escape, as far as we know, go something like this. At Le Bourget, the Paris airport, while the dancers and designers were waiting for the London flight, two Soviet agents walked up to Nureyev. He was known as Rudy, and they told him he was needed back home, that he was scheduled to perform at a Kremlin gala. And as if that weren't incentive enough they also told him his mother was sick, that she was dying, that she'd asked for him, and whenever you're given multiple reasons for acting in a certain way, it's usually an indication that the reasons are false. And Rudy, having grown up in the Soviet system, knew it. *I want to be free,* he's supposed to have said, and although he knew he might never see his mother again he took the first step. And because he was a dancer, once he took that step what he did was like dancing, like Odette slipping out of Rothbart's arms, or like any dancer, male or female, slipping out of the grip of the sorcerer or witch or malicious parent. With pirouette precision he twirled through the guards and checkpoints, performing a kind of pedestrian échappé, which literally means *escape,* but it wasn't pedestrian because he was Nureyev. And because it was 1961, during what was called the Cold War, French police were there. It's not clear how many policemen were leaning against the pillar, or what the arrangements were, but when Nureyev approached and asked them, or pleaded with them, it didn't take long before the refuge of asylum was granted. And the word *defection* is from the same root as *deficiency,* and the sense was that Rudy was leaving a deficient place, the USSR, and coming to a place with opportunity and freedom. And whether it was freedom he found on the other side of the so-called Iron Curtain or not, his move became a template for similar moves, defections by Baryshnikov and Markova, and he later partnered with Margot Fonteyn and Erik Bruhn but the hardest part was probably that first step.

The café was hot, like a jungle. Steam rose from the frying egg *foo young*, fogging up the windows and the waitress, a middle-aged woman, walked to the register, turned on the television, and since I was facing it I couldn't help watching, or at least noticing, and I knew the show, a comedy about prisoners of war. *Hogan's Heroes* was set in a German concentration camp, and it was funny because the prisoners, who could easily have escaped, chose not to escape because they'd been given a job, to fight the enemy, and I wasn't sure what my job was but I'd also chosen not to escape, to wait until our food arrived, and when it did, mostly it was brown and it sat, congealing on our plates. Nobody ate and I could tell that Sherri and Darlene weren't having fun. I'd always wanted to be the guy you could count on for fun but now here we were, not prisoners of war but we were sitting at this greasy table and the air, when people talk about air being thick it was this, like being under water, and the water was yellow, like the walls of this sad café. And I wasn't trying to be heroic but I knew the way to change the world was to change the way you *see* the world, so I took a step. Not a literal step but I said, let's go to the movies, and the girls liked that idea. We'd been sad sacks sitting in the thick café air and I was suggesting we become happy sacks, that we jump up and if it's raining, for instance, you'd be feeling wet and oppressed by the rain. But what if, like Gene Kelly in *Singin' in the Rain*, you went ahead and got wet? You let the rain infect you with its energy, and you sang and danced and the rain, which normally would have dampened your spirits, lifted your spirits. That's what I was trying to do, suggesting we go to a movie. There must be a movie theater around here, and when we left the café, walking along the sidewalk, stopping at tourist shops, looking at kites and lanterns, everything red, it wasn't that people weren't staring at us, but no one seemed to be paying us much attention. No bookie appeared as we walked to the movie theater, bought our tickets, took our seats, and since it was Chinatown, the movie was in Chinese, and because it was incomprehensible it didn't do what it was supposed to do. Our spirits weren't lifted. Instead they wandered, like the ghosts in the movie, or at least I assumed they were ghosts. They seemed to materialize at will, haunting and marauding, like creatures in a Romantic ballet except engaging in martial arts. The story seemed to revolve around a lover or brother or father who disguises himself as a woman to get inside the walls of a castle to rescue a child and kill her oppressors. And in the movie killing was easy. When people fell down they were dead. I'd heard stories about Vietnam, stories of firing blindly into the jungle, not seeing who you were shooting, and if killing has to be done, although it should never be done, it ought to be done face to face. But not by me. I could never be a person who kills, simple as that. And because I didn't want to be an accomplice to killing, although the movie wasn't over, I stood up and we filed out of our empty row and out of the empty theater. And it was strange because, when we'd walked into the theater it was daylight, and the movie had been shot in the daylight, and maybe the change I was looking for wasn't a change in myself but a change in the light, like the expression *I see daylight*, except now there was just the neon night. Which meant the show could go on.

Odette runs out of the ballroom. She's warned Siegfried not to follow her but he has to, he loves her, and she runs back to the pond, to the clearing where they first fell in love and she waits for him by a fallen branch. When he finds her he tells her that everything is fine, or is going to be fine, the kind of thing you say to a child but she believes in the curse, a ridiculous curse that Siegfried doesn't understand. I want to apologize, he says, and he does, repeatedly, hoping that if she believes in his love she can use that love to change her life. And of course she forgives him, it was no one's fault, but the spell can't be broken, she says. But I don't believe in spells. The only spell I believe is saying I love you, telling her he loves her, over and over, as if by saying that, like an incantation, the curse on her will lift. And by holding her. Remember when we held each other? But when he tries to reenact the moment from their past she steps away from him. She just doesn't want to be touched. Touching would lead to feeling, and as much as she might desire that feeling, it can't happen. It? I remember my wife telling me, after our daughter had died, it can't go on, I can't love you anymore. Which I didn't understand at the time. I was focused on my own loss and my own sadness, but I understand now, I think, that as much as she wanted to love me, she couldn't be that person anymore, the person she had been. And I understand, or said I did, which seemed to calm her down. We weren't arguing anymore, just talking, and I thought there might be hope.

It seemed we had a chance, if we wanted to take it, to wake up, realize we were in a dream, or the nightmare part of a dream, and I was still hoping we could step out of the dream when the other swans, the girls who aren't swans now but will be when daylight comes, gather around Odette. And that's when Odette suddenly rushes into the water. It seems sudden, even to her, as if her body had spoken to her, and when she heard it she did what her body demanded. And because she wasn't a swan anymore and she couldn't float, she died. Pavlova, when she danced in *The Dying Swan*, wasn't playing the part of Odette, but she was letting her body, her swanlike body, tell her what to do. It's a wholly different ballet, choreographed by Michel Fokine, who worked for Diaghilev. And it's short, one that Pavlova performed in cities around the world. And like *Swan Lake*, it's full of sadness, but also there's joy, the joy of release, of finally releasing the false self and becoming another self, not necessarily better, but by dying Pavlova becomes more who she is. Like Odette, she's trapped in the guise of a swan, and when she dies she's liberated, that overused word, but that's what she felt, what Odette felt and Fonteyn felt, and Pierina Legnani felt it when she created the role a hundred years ago. Over the course of those years the story of *Swan Lake* has mutated into various versions with various endings and usually Rothbart, who probably loved Odette, like a father or a lover, and wants her for himself, is killed by Siegfried. Sometimes Odette, as a swan, flies off into the morning sky, leaving Siegfried alone, consumed by grief. The pictures in my daughter's ballet book showed the two lovers, united in death, rising up from the watery mist like spirits. In Russia, in Soviet times, Rothbart, watching the lovers bid their last farewells, to each other and to life, and seeing the honesty of their love, removes the curse and the curtain falls with everyone living happily after. I prefer the version when Siegfried, realizing that the only way he can be with Odette is to follow her into the pond, not to save her but to end his own life, a life he knows and is tired of, does that. And we don't see the thrashing of the water as they try to swallow the water, fighting against the human body's prime directive, which is to live. We only see first their heads, disappearing under the surface of the water, a few bubbles floating up, and then the surface becomes like glass, like a mirror, reflecting the distant mountains as the sun slowly rises.

Petrushka

P etrushka is a puppet. As is the woman he loves, the Ballerina. What stands between them are a lot of things, but one of them is a character named Charlatan, or *the* Charlatan. He's both a magician and an impresario, and the show he presents in the town's central square is an old one. He brings puppets to life. When he pulls back the curtain of his makeshift stage there they are, the Moor, the Ballerina, and Petrushka, hanging lifeless from hooks. When the crowd presses closer he plays his flute and the puppets, freeing themselves from the hooks they've been hanging on, begin performing a dumbshow in which Petrushka's love of the Ballerina gets him beaten up by the Moor. It's always the same show, with the same plot, and the helpless puppets have no choice but to do what they do.

I was sitting at the Crazy Horse bar, on a bar stool, with an unobstructed view of the stage. Mr. Sophistication was under his spotlight, sitting on his stool, speaking into the microphone with a fake Viennese accent. It was Viennese because the show was the Vienna number and Teddy, wearing his top hat, cane in hand, was thanking the audience for sharing with him a modicum of pleasure on this, his tour of la Ville Lumière, the City of Light. Oh no, he said, that's Paris, and as the audience laughed the music swelled, and his song began. *Falling in love again, never wanted to, what was I to do* . . . My view of the stage included the silhouetted torsos of the customers, drinking and cheering, blowing smoke in the air, some of them laughing, most of them silently watching the dancers and waiting. I felt the sticky bar on the skin of my forearm, the rung of the stool pressing into my foot, doing what they call nursing my drink. Sherri was up on stage, along with a red-haired dancer I didn't know, and after the last *Falling in love again, never wanted to, what was I to do,* after he whispered into his microphone the last word, *helpless,* the lights dimmed. The performers disappeared behind the curtain and the intermission music, which was intended to make conversation impossible, did, and I ordered another drink from Sonny, the bartender.

Like the Scarecrow in *The Wizard of Oz,* the puppets in Petrushka have a life outside the show they perform in. It's a truncated life but it's all they know, and it's truncated because it's just the three of them. They each have a small backstage apartment where they live, and the lives they live are replicas of the lives they perform. Petrushka can't stop loving the Ballerina, who finds him pathetic. She's attracted to the handsome Moor who despises anything pathetic, especially Petrushka. And being despised, Petrushka retreats to his room, like a cell, like a jail cell except worse because he has no visitors, only the Charlatan, and although he thinks he hates the Charlatan it's his own life he really hates, and because the Charlatan is responsible for that life, or lack of life, for his weakness and his inability to woo the Ballerina, between his shows Petrushka sits in his room, on the floor, under a life-size portrait of the Charlatan, imagining

himself killing the Charlatan, living with the Ballerina, sometimes writing in his diary and always going a little mad, banging
his head against the walls of his room, cursing the person who
makes him be who he is.

Mr. Sophistication was pathetic, a fool and a clown but at least
he knew it. And the art of the clown is convincing the audience, when they look at him, that they aren't looking at themselves. That's why they put up with Teddy. It's why their booing,
while they waited for him, was affectionate. It's why Teddy, behind the mask of Mr. Sophistication, could be himself. The audience was booing as the music faded and Cosmo, in his usual
tuxedo, stepped up to the stage. He did his welcome-to-the-
club routine, told a few jokes and then he introduced the next
show, the Tokyo number. Teddy peeked out from behind the
curtains, parted the curtains, and when he walked to the microphone, once Cosmo had left the stage the music faded up and it
all seemed improvised. As Teddy began his spiel the dancers appeared, and they seemed to be making it up but their lines were
all memorized. Teddy began with a short historical digression,
about the ancient Japanese city of Edo and the masks of the Noh
theater, and Darlene was playing the part of a concubine. It was
her duet with Teddy, and wearing an extremely thin kimono she
bowed to him. And because they were pretending to be in Japan,
Teddy bowed to her, a little lower, and she then bowed to him a
little lower and they kept that up, deferentially bowing to each
other, lower and lower, and because Teddy was facing the audience and she was facing Teddy, her ass, with its sparkling decorations, was presented to the audience. People were half drunk
and cheering, and I was distracted by a dream I'd had in which

I was in a boat, a small rowboat. The Commodore, in the bow of the boat, was ordering me to row, to pull and pull, and because my back was facing forward I couldn't see where we were going and then I felt a hand on my shoulder. When I came out of the dream the show was still going on, and the hand on my shoulder, which wasn't a dream, was connected to Seymour. It was Seymour's hand, and when I turned I saw on his face his smile, and although it was absolutely believable, I didn't believe it. Because it was too believable. It was too wide, the teeth too white, and it didn't leave his face when he asked me if I'd found the Chinaman. There was a discontinuity or disparity or disunity between what was happening on the surface of his teeth, which were white, and what happening in his eyes, or actually in my heart when I looked into his eyes, which was darkness. We went to Chinatown, I told him. But we didn't find the bookie. And I've given it some thought, I said, and I'm not interested in finding this bookie anymore. I've had a change of plans. I've decided to pay back the loan in a regular way, in installments, and his eyes were still empty, and his mouth was still full of teeth when he asked me to join him outside. Sorry, I told him, I can't. I'm watching the show and the show's not over. Seymour, pulling at his mustache as if he was caressing a pet, a small rodent, said, just for a few minutes. You can spare a few minutes. And as he said it I felt his fingers grip my upper arm and he pulled my arm. After you, he said, and he pulled me off my stool and I signaled to Sonny that I'd be right back, not that he cared but I wanted a witness. And his fingers on my arm, as they pulled on me, made me feel like a girl, a young girl, an innocent girl and Seymour was putting the moves on her. He led me outside and we walked past the lights of the LIVE NUDE GIRLS sign, down to a doorway where it wasn't so bright, where Freddie seemed to be waiting. As if they were passing me off. Freddie, who was quite a bit bigger than I was, placed his arm around my neck as if cradling my head, and he walked me across the street, dodging the cars driving up and down the street, and he led me into a concrete parking garage. He took me to the elevator doors, which opened, and he took me to the second floor, and when we stepped out into the darkness he finally spoke. You know what's going to happen, right? And I didn't. Until he asked me the question. And when I looked at his eyes they actually seemed to have some sympathy. His teeth were crooked but his eyes were expressing, not a sadness for himself but a sadness for me, and I was about to respond to his sadness with a smile, or a plea, and that's when he threw his fist into my stomach. Because it was unexpected my stomach, when he hit it, the muscles that might normally have tensed to protect me were soft, and his hard fist sunk into my belly, into my intestines, deep enough that I doubled over or tried to double over but he took hold of my hair. He lifted my head by the hair and hit me again, again in the stomach, in the umbilical region, the place where, long ago, I was connected to my mother. And I don't know how many times he hit me there, and he slapped my face, and I suppose when he thought I'd gotten the point he lifted me by the collar of my shirt, like I was a puppet, and he pulled me back to the elevator, down to the street, and across the street, and he pushed me into a car, a Cadillac.

The characters in *Petrushka*, because they have consciousness, don't believe they're puppets. They know they occasionally put on a show, but the lives they lead outside the show, however circumscribed, are completely real to them. The emotions they feel, the love and hate, although they're puppet emotions, are the same ones we all feel. Or I do. Petrushka's desire to create a new life, to escape the life he's somehow gotten himself into, is perfect for breaking his heart, and it was breaking my heart but because it was the only life I knew there was nothing I could do. I thought I hated the Commodore, and I probably did, but what motivated my hate was the fact that I hated myself for being a puppet.

I was sitting in the front seat of the Cadillac, between the accountant, on the driver's side, and Freddie, on the passenger side, who was patting my thigh, saying to me, bravo, you made it. The Commodore, Seymour, and the crew-cut guy were sitting in the backseat and the car was parked in front of the club. They weren't negotiating at this point, or suggesting, they were telling me what I had to do. And partly because I'd been beaten up, and partly because they were all talking at the same time, giving me instructions, although they were probably all speaking complete sentences, I heard their words like a kaleidoscope, or like a Cubist painting, the various parts all represented but none of the parts were in the right place. Or in the normal place. I didn't know who said what but I was told about where the Chinese guy had his clubhouse or fortress, about the henchmen or bodyguards who lived in an A-frame house in front of this fortress. I was told about the dogs I'd have to placate, and how to placate them, with meat, and what breed they were, Doberman, and they asked me which gun. What? Which gun did I want to use. I was offered a choice. They had a .45 caliber and a .38, and my choice wasn't about whether to use the gun to kill the bookie, it was about which gun I preferred to use. That I was killing the Chinese bookie was a given, kill him or

something happens to me, and Freddie advised me to use the
.38 caliber because a .38 never jams. I'd only touched a handful
of guns in my life, but I picked the .45 because forty-five de-
grees is a right angle and he pulled one out of the glove com-
partment. It was wrapped in white cloth. When you're done
with the gun, Seymour said, wipe it and throw it away. I put
the gun, which was heavy, in my pocket, and then they told me
about my vehicle. They'd procured a car for me, stolen it, and it
was hot-wired so Freddie warned me not to stall. Seymour, in
the backseat, opened a map, pointed to marks on the map but
it was dark in the car, plus the map was upside down. Take the
freeway past Ventura Boulevard, he said, go under the bridge
and get off at Rossmore, the Rossmore exit. Go three blocks up
the hill and park the car. It's all marked on the map. I took the
map and he gave me a key, and then the accountant pulled out
a manila folder. In it was a piece of paper, *the* piece of paper,
what they called my marker, signed by me, for twenty-three
thousand dollars. It's yours now, he said and he handed me the
paper and the Commodore told me to rip it up. Go ahead, he said,
you can rip it up, and after I tore the paper in half we all got
out of the Cadillac. Like a cow or a sheep, an ungulate like
that, I was herded up the street to another car, a Pontiac. It
wasn't a Bonneville and it wasn't new, but I was told, this is your
baby, which made everyone laugh. I didn't laugh but I got in the
car, which was running, and there wasn't a key, just some wires
hanging down under the dashboard. Seymour opened the passenger door, bent over as if he was going to tell me something,
some last instruction, and then he smiled, shut the door, and
waved to me through the window. Then they all walked away.
And then there was nothing to do but shift into drive, take my

foot off the brake, ease out of the parking spot, and the only direction to go was forward so I drove in that direction. I could see them in the rearview mirror watching me drive off, and the direction I was going had been decided for me, and was it the direction of happiness? Or the direction of actually killing someone? I didn't have time to think about that. The first thing to think about was surviving, and then the second thing and the third and fourth and everything else follows from that. You make adjustments to where you thought you were going, and who you thought you were, and this is my direction, I thought, the direction I find myself going, and what I have to do, or what I have to be, or somehow what I am, is ahead of me.

Before he was a famous choreographer Vaslav Nijinsky was a dancer. In 1911 he danced the original *Petrushka*, choreographed by Michel Fokine, and in it he incorporated all the entrechats and échappés that were part of traditional ballet, but he went beyond that. He let his body jerk and convulse, his toes pointing in instead of classically out, and although some considered it unbecoming, it was perfect for expressing the sadness of Petrushka's struggle. Nijinsky felt the sadness because in his own life he was struggling for control, and because he was losing the struggle, the madness that would later take over his life was already evident. He was, for a time, Diaghilev's lover, and referring to Diaghilev in his diary he says, *I began to hate him quite openly, and once I pushed him on a street in Paris. I pushed him because I wanted to show him that I was not afraid of him. . . . I pushed him only slightly because I felt not anger . . . but tears.* When, as Petrushka, he sat alone in his room he would soothe himself by imagining the ballerina he loved, caressing her imaginary body and then his own body, touching himself like a child who's learning to pleasure herself, and I say *her*self because he danced in a way that crossed the line between male and female. Like a lot of dancers he was androgynous, and he was able, according to his wife, to place himself in the soul of a woman. And because his soul was full of sexuality, and because his sexuality was part of his madness, when he exhibited his madness on stage his performances were scandalous. In his diary he talks of his struggle with chastity and with vegetarianism, and he records, along with his bowel movements, a variety of sexual fantasies. And when those who supposedly loved him, and probably did love him, wanted to cure him of these fantasies, he didn't understand. *I will not be put in a lunatic asylum, because I dance very well and give money to anyone who asks me.* He was a human being, and human beings have thoughts, both known and unknown, and psychologists refer to schizophrenia as a breakdown in selective attention, meaning that a person, in the middle of a thought, makes a connection with another thought, which connects to another, and they seem like random associations, which is why it's called madness, but sometimes it's called the only way to deal with a situation.

Your dancers are like the artist's tubes of paint, with the great difference that they must be both willing and receptive. That's what Haskell says, and I don't know about the artist's tubes of paint but when I pulled out of the parking space, drove down Hollywood Boulevard and merged onto the freeway, I was like a tributary joining the current of a larger river. Freeway driving, at night, was always relaxing, the taillights in front of me, the headlights behind me, and since I was already driving south, whether it was inertia or my fighting inertia, I decided to keep going, all the way to Mexico. I could live off the land down there, that's the expression, take my life into my own hands, which was what I thought I was doing. I literally had my hands on the steering wheel, and although the seat was uncomfortable and my stomach was sore, knowing where I was going was pleasant. And driving on the freeway was pleasant, something I'd done a thousand times. Not in this particular car, but in any car you hold the wheel, one foot on the gas, mirrors looking back at the receding world, windshield displaying the approaching world, and as a driver you're in the middle, not part of the past where you've been, and not quite yet to the place you're going, and not knowing what will happen when you get there. The hum of the engine, and the hum of the tires on the road, and the hum in the back of my brain, or the buzz, whatever it was I found it soothing, hypnotic but not soporific, and that's when I heard the pop. The tire. The right front tire exploded like a popping tire and the car was suddenly hard to steer. The engine lost power and the car slowed down and it wasn't just the tire. The gas pedal didn't seem to be affecting the pistons, which stopped humming, and smoke began seeping out from under the hood, up near the tire but not the tire, billowing back to the windshield and making it hard to see. And then the car stopped moving. And there was no key to start it again, if it would start, and I was in the middle lane of a three-lane freeway, cars passing on my left and right, and the cars behind me were swerving around me, the pitch of their horns rising and falling in what I thought was the Doppler effect. And because the lights of the car turned off when the engine turned off, it was possible the cars approaching from behind, not seeing the car, would hit the car, so I waited until there was a relative break in traffic, then I opened my door, ran around the dead car and it must've been a four-lane freeway because I had to cross two lanes to get to the shoulder, that's what they called it, not that I counted them, I had to dodge the oncoming lights. And trucks were also on the road, long multi-wheeled trucks and my car was out there, a smoking piece of metal, waiting to be hit, or explode, and I wasn't asking myself what I was doing. I wasn't thinking about Mexico, or crossing the border, or killing someone. Thoughts were entering my stream of thoughts but the stream was moving too fast to actually stop the thoughts and hold them in my mind. All my life it's been other people, the Commodore or the Charlatan or whoever it was they were thinking my thoughts, and I didn't think because I never had time, although I could have made time, but now my heart was beating too fast. My blood was doing the thinking now, moving inside my veins or my vessels, or both of them, stretching those veins and I was just doing what it told me to do, which was, first of all, breathe. I was standing on the gravel at the side of the nighttime freeway, the dust whirling in eddies as the cars sped past, and of all the thoughts I might have thought the one I started thinking was, I should raise the hood of the Pontiac. The emblem of a Pontiac was an image of Chief Pontiac, in silhouette, long hair, strong shoulders, and it wasn't because of Chief Pontiac, but I decided I should alert the passing drivers that an obstruction existed. A flare would've been ideal but I didn't have a flare, so I waited for a lull in the traffic, or to be poetic, in the ribbon of cars, the lights like a ribbon of crystal, or more like a necklace, or really more like water, that old standby, the freeway becoming a river like everything seems to become a river, a fast-moving river in this case, and I waded across the current of the river, got to the front of the Pontiac, unlatched the hood, lifted it up, and because it was dark the car was invisible, and therefore vulnerable, so I ran back to the shoulder. Cars were passing, their horns blaring, and instead of staying put and waiting for help to arrive, or police to arrive, I started running. There was an exit up ahead and I ran past the plastic cups and matted socks and mainly it was dirt, and I ran along the guardrail at the side of the freeway until I came to an off-ramp. I followed its spiraling slope down to a fairly deserted part of the city, nothing open at this hour except a gas station, an Economy Self-Serve, and I wasn't running, I was walking now, past the pumps to an area with water hoses and air for tires. I stepped inside a phone booth next to the bathroom, and when I shut the phone booth door a fluorescent light above my head turned on.

Like me, Petrushka had been given a chance to escape. Like me, he'd been a good boy, going along with the program as they say, allowing himself to be used by the people who did the using, and there was no ballerina to distract me, and no Moor to beat me, and when the operator came on the line I asked for a cab. I didn't care which one. Able Cab or A-1 Cab or ABC. I told the dispatcher where I was and then I made another call, to the Crazy Horse. It was Cosmo I was calling, not sure what I was going to tell him or ask him, not sure if I was going to ask him anything. What should I do? I could've asked him that. Or what *can* I do? That's more like it. Either way, it was putting my life in Cosmo's hands, which I was trying not to do, but when Sonny picked up the phone I asked him if Cosmo was home. I said *home* but I meant in the club, and Sonny said what sounded like yes, but the connection was bad and I said, can I talk to him?

Fine, he said, go ahead. No, I said, can I talk to Cosmo? Put Cosmo on the line. I could hear in the background a show going on, the Vienna number it sounded like, and I said, how's the show? There was a pause on the line. Cosmo? Is that you? But Sonny must have put the phone on the bar, the black phone on the dark bar next to the rag that wiped the bar, and I said into my end of the phone, Hello? I was thinking someone would hear me. Hello? And it was definitely the Vienna number. Teddy's ersatz Austrian accent was audible in the background, and I was trying to figure out, from what Mr. Sophistication was saying, where they were in the number, expecting to hear Cosmo's voice on the phone any second. Cosmo? Is anyone there? I enunciated my words. Can anyone hear me? Teddy was singing now, *Falling in love again*, and I found myself singing along, *never wanted to*, like Marlene Dietrich, *what was I to do*, singing into the receiver attached to the cord attached to the booth, standing under the sharp fluorescent light. I was looking across at the gas station pumps, the freeway behind me, and I didn't know who was on the other end of the line but I was singing to him, or her, that there was nothing I could do, that I was helpless, and then a cab pulled up in front of the phone booth and I hung up. When I walked to the cab I kept my head down, as if it was raining, but it wasn't raining, and when the cabbie, without looking in his mirror, asked me where I was going, I told him I'd know where it was when I saw it.

The Moor has invited the Ballerina into his room. It's a lavish room, with hookahs and rugs and the Moor doesn't know about love, or care, but because the Ballerina is flirting with him he responds with the kind of aggressiveness she pretends not to like but obviously does. She plays a toy trumpet for him, seductively. She dances for him in her seductive costume. She sits on his lap, and there used to be an expression, *heavy petting*, and that's what they're doing when Petrushka throws open the door. He's a Pierrot, a character that originated in the commedia dell'arte, and like any Pierrot, when he falls in love he falls deeply. And like Pierrot, when it comes to expressing that love, he's a buffoon. He's full of hope and naïveté, and because the Ballerina enjoys attention she encourages his, toying with his affection until, losing interest in the game, which is her game, she dismisses him. Which doesn't make sense to him because he loves her. And feeling that love, unless there's an object to absorb that love, to relish it and possibly return it, the love, having nowhere to go it, starts to drive you crazy. And that's when the Ballerina turns from him, turning her attention to the handsome Moor.

I was sitting at the bar at a neighborhood bar and grill, not drinking a drink because what I needed now was meat. And this particular bar had a takeout menu, and hamburgers were on the menu, and that's why I was talking to the waitress. What can I get you, she said, and I said, twelve hamburgers, and she was quick. Having a party? I was sitting on a stool, facing forward, and she was to my right and I didn't respond to her joke because what did it mean that I ordered the meat? That I was going through with this? My errand. I wasn't necessarily going through with anything. One step at a time, that's all I was taking. One small step didn't necessarily lead to a leap, and because the bar wasn't busy she stood there, with her weight on one foot, and I told her, no ketchup and no mustard. And no buns. You just want the meat of twelve hamburgers. She said it not as a question but as a way, by repeating the words, to get them to make sense. The bartender was washing glasses behind the bar but she seemed to be the person on duty, and normally, after writing down my order she would've delivered it to the kitchen where they would've cooked up whatever she'd written but now she wasn't moving. She managed a small smile. How do you want your meat? Rare, I told her, trying to be as clear as I could. I didn't say raw because, although dogs like raw meat, maybe I wouldn't be feeding the dogs. Maybe the actions I was taking wouldn't lead to other actions made possible by the first action, and she wanted to know if I wanted my buns on the side. She'd be happy to wrap them. Her mascara was blue, and she was lingering over my order, not because it was complicated but she was making it complicated. Let's see, she said. Twelve hamburgers, no lettuce, tomato, ketchup, no mustard, and no buns. That's it, I said, and I noticed the smile that had been on her face had gotten replaced with the musculature of a smile, a mask she maintained as she turned and walked to the kitchen with my order. Leaving me alone on my stool. And it took a second before I noticed the warmth of the bar. It was smoke filled, humming with the noise of jukebox songs and ice cubes and conversations that had nothing to do with me. And it was soothing, letting the conversations swirl around me, letting my limbs get soft and my thoughts, about the job I was supposed to be doing, get replaced by other thoughts. Which is why I could easily imagine myself stepping off the bar stool, and there was a phone booth in the bar, against a wall by some tables, and I seem to have walked to the booth and now I'm sitting on a small folding table, reaching up and sliding my quarter in the slot. I say *seem* because, although my thoughts are like memories they aren't memories, which is why I have to imagine them. And when I hear the ringing on the other end, when she picks up, I know why I'm calling. And the chitchat is part of the dream, I guess, and my ex-wife had a name but I'm not calling her, I'm calling my daughter. And my daughter is busy, that's what I'm told, and I can hear my ex-wife's lack of interest as she questions me about what I've been doing, and nothing, I tell her because what's the point. And then my daughter comes on the line. Hers is the voice I need to remember, filled with life, and the curiosity of life, and she wants to know what I'm doing, right now. I tell her, I'm talking to you, which I am, and I ask her what she is doing right now. Her toys. Her grandmother gave her some Russian dolls, and she starts explaining how one doll lives inside another which fits inside another, and language was still new to her and her voice, I wish I remembered it better but I remember its innocence and its purity, and her love, which was also pure, was the only love I've ever been completely sure of, hers for me and mine for her, and it wasn't just the reciprocity of love, although that was part of it. It was the moment in my life when joy existed for me, as an offering, and because I didn't appreciate it then, or didn't know I appreciated it, I can't just let go of it. And *it* won't let go of me. Even after all these years I feel it, expanding in my chest, and I could say expanding like warm steam but it's not like anything. It's her, and I listen to her unpack her wooden dolls, breaking them apart, and now I'll put them together, she says, describing her work, so serious, and she was always serious. When she was a baby I would watch her maneuvering her way through what must have been an unknown universe, the first human soul to walk and eat and figure out which shoe went on which foot. And everything we do becomes a habit, including the habit of not paying attention, which is why I'm paying attention now, to this angel, my child, and it's also myself I want to remember, and because I feel her inside me I can hear, in the singsong intonation of her voice, the life I can't forget. And I refuse to forget. Or say good-bye. But I have to, that's what time does, and knowing the conversation has to end, and because it has to end, although I would like to stay inside this phone booth forever, that's when the waitress tapped my shoulder. And now it's over. The waitress was back and phone booth is gone and now I was back in the world of the waitress. There seemed to be a problem with my order. Not a problem but my hamburgers weren't ready. She wasn't sure she'd gotten my order right. She knew what people ordered in a bar and grill, and twelve pieces of hamburger meat wasn't it. I was either joking with her or she wasn't hearing me right, and although she seemed to want to understand, it was more like a refusal to understand, and to get the idea to lodge in her brain I had to be the kind of guy who wasn't the kind of guy I was. Cosmo had been that kind of guy and now I was standing, looking down at her brown hair, my voice rising in intensity, and because she was friendly she assumed that I would be friendly, or hoped I would be, a reciprocity that might normally get her through the day or night but I didn't have time for reciprocity. I told her to cook my fucking hamburgers. I don't give a fuck about fucking condiments or fucking buns, and maybe I didn't say *fucking* quite that much, but when I told her to get her goddamned nose out of my business, although I noticed moisture near her blue mascara, I had to do what I was doing. I had to get to my destination, wherever that was, and I wasn't yelling, but whatever I said, when I said it, I could see the moisture coalescing into almost a tear, a tear she probably tried to hold back but couldn't. And the bartender had been listening like bartenders listen, with one ear, but one ear was enough, and I wanted to get this over with so, fine, I said, the buns. I'll take the buns. And when I said it she smiled, a smile of relief, an honest smile this time and I sat on the bar stool, my arms on the bar, my eyes looking down at the water stains or beer stains or the circular mark of a glass on the grain of the wood in front of me. And when the burgers arrived the grease was already leaking into the brown paper bag. I paid the bartender because the waitress was busy, or pretending to be busy, and I went outside, dumped the buns in a garbage can, and the cab I'd told to wait for me was waiting at the curb.

The only way Petrushka can escape his situation is to die. So he thought. He knew the Ballerina would never love him and the Charlatan would never free him, and that's fine. I've been a puppet all my life. I can't just suddenly change who I am or leave who I am, it doesn't happen like that. I don't want to die, but if dying is the only way to escape my fate, or my future, or whatever it is, I'll do it. What do I have that's so precious to lose? My life as a puppet? A pathetic puppet incapable of love, although that's not right. I have known love. But at some point you have to say, well, that was nice, that life I knew, but it's over. And the music for the ballet is by Igor Stravinsky, but I wasn't hearing the music because I was in the cab, and the cab's radio was tuned to a station that was talking about traffic. I was riding in the cab to the house of a Chinese person. I was partly excited and partly I was numb. I had a gun in my pocket which was exciting, but what I was going to do with the gun, that was the numb part, the puppet part, as if what I did wasn't done by me. It was done by a man holding a greasy bag of meat, half-cooked, holding it in his open palm so the bag, if it broke, wouldn't stain his clothes. I'd never wanted to play the role of this man but now I'd been given the role and that's what you do, you come out of the womb and it starts like that, being told what you are, what you can be, and maybe you like it and maybe you don't but either way you stop thinking about the role because not thinking makes it easier. And when we got to a corner at the base of a hill I told the driver to stop. I gave him some money, watched him drive off, and from the corner I began walking up the deserted street. I did it quietly, avoiding the circles of light cast by the streetlights. And the walk, which wasn't long, reminded me of a walk I'd taken with my aunt, a hike, a Sierra Club hike up a hill. I was young so I got to the top of the hill before the older ladies, imagining myself an explorer, the first human soul to ever stand under this particular pine tree, on these particular needles, and it was a different location now but the soundlessness was the same. It was a soundlessness in which I felt my heart beat, and sometimes I chewed gum to keep calm, and I didn't have any gum but I had a cigar in my pocket. The coat I was wearing was Cosmo's coat, an old one he'd given me, and the cigar in the pocket was Cosmo's cigar. I held it between my lips, not lighting it because the ember would call attention to the man walking up to the tall wooden gate, and on the other side of the gate he heard the dogs. And they heard him. And I pulled the meat, half wrapped in wax paper, from the brown bag, and maybe I should have kept the buns. It would have been easier, or cleaner, because now I reached into the bag, grabbed the half-cooked hamburger and dropped it over the gate. Through a slit between the gate and the fence I counted two dogs, and I could see the meat hit the cement and the dogs attacking it. First they sniffed it, then attacked it, and they didn't care if the meat was cooked or not. Dobermans tend to be tailless, or stub tailed, because people cut the tails off, and when the meat was gone, and the violence of the growling was gone, I pulled the metal wire that released the gate, pushed it slowly open, said calming things to the dogs, nice dog, good doggy, things like that, and the dogs sniffed me but I wasn't meat, or not the kind of meat they liked. They seemed sated, their jaws resting on the cement near a stainless steel water bowl, and they let me squeeze past them. I walked along the side of a stucco house, into an open area that led to an unpaved road, a private road, and I walked up that until, about a hundred feet ahead of me I saw the A-frame house. Then I tossed the cigar. I'd been told there would be bodyguards, and I saw them, three or four figures moving back and forth in front of a large triangular window. The window overlooked the road which had turned into a path, and as I walked below the A-frame house I was acting the part of someone who knows where he's going. If they stopped me I'd say I'm . . . I'd make something up. People tend to let you keep walking if you walk with purpose and that's how I walked up the path, hearing the voices of the henchmen coming from the window. The language they spoke, I assumed, was Chinese, and I could feel the weight of the key against my thigh, the key I'd been given, and I walked up some paving-stone stairs to another level and there was a house here, a bigger house. I passed an open doorway, and because I was trying to walk with purpose I hardly turned my head but inside the door I saw a group of people in a room, a family, kids and women in yellow light, and I kept walking, around the house to the back stairs. From the top of the stairs, hearing the voices of the family below me, the kids laughing and the adults laughing too, it sounded like a family that probably knew love. But I couldn't afford to think about that. I had to think about what I was doing, and the act of killing, although I didn't think about that, must have meant something to me because I had to block from my mind the happiness of the family. I pulled out the key to the door and when the key opened the door I stepped inside. It was dark in the room when I closed the door but I noticed a light down one hallway, and voices. I followed the sound of the voices to a half-open door that led to what looked like a bathroom but bigger, like a steam room. It was a tiled room with a large tiled tub and sitting in the tub, his back toward me, was a thin, gray-haired man. Next to him, facing him, a small young girl with long dark hair was laughing. They were both laughing, flirting with each other by splashing each other, and from what I could see she wasn't wearing a top. The man was distracted, enjoying her attention, and this would be the perfect moment, I thought, the back of his head a perfect target. *Would* be the perfect moment, if what I was going to do was kill him. But I wasn't sure I was. I didn't think I was. Or mainly I wasn't thinking. The gun was still in the pocket of my coat, and now, with the perfect moment directly in front of me, I left it there, waiting until I knew what I was doing. Or until a more perfect, perfect moment came along, and as is often the case, by waiting for a better moment the moment that was perfectly fine slipped away. Which would have been perfect for me. I could've gone back to the Commodore and told him . . . I didn't know what, and I was thinking about what it might be when the girl slipped out from under the old man's arms. She stepped out of the tub, walked to a lacquered liquor cabinet, mixed herself a drink, and instead of walking back to the old man she walked into what looked like a bathroom. And then the old man, naked, his skin hanging off his bones like the skin of an old hound, stood. He didn't see me watching him step out of the tub and walk across the tiled floor, and when he got to a door he stopped. I didn't know where the door might lead but this, I thought, must be the perfect moment. He was dizzy, or he was thinking, either way he was defenseless, his rib cage visible, his scapula sticking out, and I was close enough to hit the back of his head if I shot him. And that's when the thought of shooting him, a thought I'd been able to avoid until then, hit me. Along with the abstract concept of killing, there was the concrete image of the contents of his skull splattering across the white door in front of him. And I wasn't ready for that. I wasn't ready for him to never again splash water on his girlfriend. Or even if she was a prostitute I wasn't ready, and I had no intention of being ready, and I would've turned and walked down the hall and out the door and back to my puppet self, but my puppet self was already here. The man, if he'd been a Tai Chi master, would have heard my breathing or sensed my heat, and if he'd been having a heart attack, that would've made it easy but then he opened the door. He reached out, turned the handle, and without looking back he stepped into another room and closed the door behind him.

Nijinsky, when he danced the role of Petrushka, accentuated the character's madness, which was *his* madness. No one noticed because madness gave his dancing power, made him a genius, *le dieu de la danse*, and it wasn't until he stopped dancing, or started dancing less, that his mind, which was subjugated to his body, began to spin out of control. In his diary he made no distinc-

tion between God's voice and his own voice because he saw no
distinction. And when he danced Petrushka he let his madness
speak, unafraid of what it said or why he said it, and people loved
the dancing but the madness was frightening. It was frightening because the chances he took weren't the chances they wanted
to take. But they wanted *him* to take them. They wanted him
to open his eyes and see the connections they were unwilling to
see, but had to see, and I could have opened my own eyes, seen
what I was doing or about to do but again, a moment in which I
don't act came, and then it was gone. I was still in the one room
and the old man had entered the other room, and I didn't know
what he was doing in that room, possibly preparing to ambush
me, and the girl was probably taking a shower, and all I had to
do was remember my job. I waited a few seconds, and then I quietly turned the handle of the door, and when I very cautiously
stepped inside I saw in the room a large pool, a swimming pool,
and I saw the old man stepping down into the shallow end of
the pool. The light was blue, sparkling in the water, and this was
the moment I pulled out the pistol. The water in the hot tub had
been hot water and this was cool water and the man took off his
glasses, set them on the edge of the pool, dipped his head under
the water, pushed off and glided, not like a fish but not like an
old man either. I stepped to the pool's edge, and he was graceful
under the water, holding his breath, his skinny legs propelling
him forward, and the whole pool must have been shallow because when he stood up at the deep end he was still only crotch
deep, and standing there he wiped the water out of his face. And
once he did he saw me, facing him, holding a gun. I was standing
on the beige tile, expecting him to call out to his bodyguards but
instead he said something to me, matter-of-factly, staring at me

as if I ought to understand but he spoke Chinese. You're making a big mistake, or You don't have to do this to me, or more like, So this is the day I am going to die. I couldn't think about what he was saying because if I started thinking I wouldn't cock the gun. I wouldn't hear the click when I pulled back the slide, and when I extended my arm with the gun in my hand, both of his arms were hanging at his sides. He continued staring, either at me, or it looked as if he was staring at something in front of me, something between us, something passing from him to me or me to him, and in a movie my character would talk to him, say something to him that would give him a chance to prepare for death but this wasn't a movie. I'd come this far so now my finger pulled the trigger. That was the next step, and I say *my finger* because my finger seemed to make the decision, not me, and it was just the one shot. I'd been looking at the dark spots of his two eyes so I didn't know where I'd hit him but one shot seemed to be enough. He fell back into the water and the water parted for him. And gradually, as the waves of his splash died down his body rose up, floating on the water, his feet pulling him down but his lungs were still filled with air. His blood was staining the water, spreading out, and his thin hair was spread across on the surface of the water, and that's when I heard the girl. I turned, and she was older than a girl, and she was standing at the open door, and when she turned and ran off, that's when I heard the footsteps on the stairs. Although I hadn't noticed it, the sound of the shot had probably been loud, and by the time the henchmen, two of them, rushed into the room I'd followed the girlfriend back into the hot-tub room, and then down the hall, and there was light from the open door but mostly the room was dark, and I listened. I heard splashing as the bodyguards pulled their boss's body back to shore, and no one else seemed to be running into the room so I walked out the door. From the top of the stairs I saw people running below me, some with dogs on leashes, and voices were calling to other voices, and in the confusion of barking voices I ran down the stairs, past the room where the family had been, down the path past the A-frame house, and it would have been a perfectly clean getaway except about halfway to the gate I noticed a sensation in my side, below my ribs. But I kept running. I got to the gate, opened it, ran down the street to another street, ran down that to a busy street with stores and lights and on the corner a bus had stopped to pick up passengers. I got on the bus, walked to a seat in the back and sat, looking straight ahead. I was looking straight ahead, my face more or less expressionless, but in my body I was glowing with a physical sense of exultation, of floating, and it took a while before I looked down to see that I was bleeding.

It wasn't exultation, it was adrenaline, the drug, the chemical compound manufactured by the body, and it was affecting my body more than my mind because my mind, I was going to say my mind was numb but my whole puppet self was numb. I was sitting on the bright orange bus seat, holding a shiny steel pole that connected to the seat in front of me, and there's a scene in the Godard movie *Pierrot le Fou* in which the hero, a Petrushka character, travels with the woman he loves to the south of France. And when she abandons him he decides to blow himself up, literally. He crawls into a trash can, covers himself with sticks of dynamite, lights a fuse, and as the fuses start burning he thinks, wait a minute, I don't want to do this, I don't want to die, and he tries to snuff out the burning fuses but the fuses don't snuff and we see him explode, or at least we see an explosion, and when I looked down at my right side rib, the *floating* rib, below the rib my blood was seeping into my shirt. I realized, putting two and two together as they say, that one, I'd been shot, and two, the bullet seemed to have passed through my body. I couldn't remember what organ was down there, didn't know my intestine was puctured but the body can heal itself, I knew that, or thought I did, and I would be fine as long as I didn't bleed to death. And I wasn't bleeding much. And a certain bleeding is good, I thought, because bleeding would force me to focus, on the famous here and now, and mostly I was, looking down at the blood on my shirt, but also the world was out there. I looked out to the wet streets outside the bus window, a taxicab idling by a gas station phone booth. And when the bus pulled up to a bus stop I got off the bus, and it wasn't raining, and hadn't been raining, and why were the streets wet? They always seemed to be wet. And when I walked across the wet sidewalk and opened the taxi door, the painful part was sliding into the seat. I told the driver, I'm going to a movie and he said, which movie? I didn't know. Sometimes I just want to see images of people moving in front of me, that's what I said and he said he saw that every night, meaning through his windshield, and I had my right hand holding my wound. Although the painful part was my lower back, I found myself cradling my belly, the edge of it where the blood was, cupping my hand on the place where the bullet had torn me, trying to keep the wetness inside myself from leaking out. When the car hit a pothole the bump, transmitted to my body, exaggerated the pain, but I could stand the pain, and then the cabbie pulled up to the curb. It was lit by a theater marquee. This is perfect, I told him, and when I put a bill in his hand and left his cab I pretended to walk toward the theater. In case the cabbie was watching me. I pretended to read the poster for the movie, and actually I did read it, but I have no memory of what the movie was. Not *Singin' in the Rain*. Gene Kelly wasn't singin' or dancin' or falling in love in the fake rain of a movie set. And I wasn't falling in love either. But I felt a similar endorphin flowing in me, and I knew from my studies that pain, which originates in the body, is felt in the mind, like rain falling in Los Angeles, and how we feel about that rain is up to us, and pain is the same, it's just pain, and if I could feel it without fighting it, it could just be there, with me, no big thing. Not that I wanted it. Or wanted having it. But that's the role I'd been given, a lousy role, but the fact that I didn't want the role made no difference to the powers that be, the powers that are, the powers that cast me, against type, as a person who kills people. A few days ago, or hours even, although he might have dreamed about killing the Moor, Petrushka wouldn't have been able to do it. And he didn't intend to do it. He just wanted someone to look at him and pay attention, to see he wasn't a buffoon, and now here I was, and I didn't hail another cab, but when a cab pulled up to the curb I got in, and although I was wearing my same old costume I wasn't quite feeling like me anymore.

In retrospect, killing the bookie was easy. And if it would have been a crime, which it was, it would've been the perfect crime except, first of all, I was shot. And now what? I took the cab to a bar about two blocks up the street. I could have walked to the bar even with a hole in body, but I felt like splurging, like celebrating. I had my freedom now, a big word but that's what it felt like, doing what I had to do to get the weight off my chest,

and off my mind, and scotch and water. That's what I ordered.
I didn't care what brand, or what liquor even. I sat at the bar,
drank it down and ordered another, feeling both freedom and
happiness, or trying to. I tried to put on a happy face as they say,
hoping my outward expression might affect the inner tranquillity or lack of tranquillity, and I've never been good at faking a
smile, at consciously willing my lips to spread across my teeth,
as if my lips belonged to someone else and then, when I slid off
the bar stool I spilled my stupid drink. Some scotch spilled on
my cuff and my hand and I shook my hand to shake off the wetness and also to shake off the feeling that felt like the opposite of
freedom. The jukebox was playing a song, a song I didn't know
but I heard the words, *almost in love with you*. And your mood is
your mood, meaning it's malleable, you can make it be what you
want, and the song wasn't a dance song but I wanted to feel like
dancing. But everyone else just sat on their stools, *perched* is the
word, elbows lodged like fence posts into the wood of the bar
and come on, people, I said, but the joint, as they say, was dead.
So I took the rest of my scotch to a table. I sat on the worn pad-
ding of a large chair, hoping my newfound freedom would sink
in, would start to exist and then sink in and that's when someone said to me, What are you so happy about?

Me?

You're smiling.

Why not? And when I said this, the woman, in her twenties, with bangs and a handmade blouse, sitting alone in a booth
to my right, smiled. A half smile. Half of it confident, and the
other half, the not-smiling half, intrigued me. She reminded me
of someone, and I told her, as if we were friends, I feel like a mil-
lion bucks. That's what I wanted to feel like, or should have felt

like, and the fact that I didn't made it worse. I didn't tell her I'd just murdered a person. I tried to be casual. I covered the blood on my shirt with my jacket, pretending I was fine, or better than fine. I'm golden, I said, not quite knowing what that meant, but she seemed to know, or at least she responded by raising her glass, like a toast, and sure. I could feel myself getting into character. Not sure who the character was but whoever it was he started chatting with her, asking questions about her life and revealing details about his life, which was *my* life, and the details were insignificant but still, something was passing between us, and I asked this person in the handmade shirt if I might offer her a nightcap, and she laughed at that, or maybe a shoulder to cry on, whatever she might need. Her collarbones were showing. And it was cold in the bar but they do that, keep the temperature low so that people won't sleep, so they'll keep moving or keep drinking, and she wasn't a runaway, her clothes were too nice. And when I actually looked into her face I could see in her face the same kind of eagerness my daughter used to have, the same willingness Nijinksy had, to risk his common sense, and my daughter wouldn't have been as old as this girl, and didn't look like this girl, and the reason I didn't want to think about my daughter is complicated. Like everything is complicated. That's why I killed the old man, to settle my complications, and although killing someone is also a complication, I thought I'd settled my debt. Now I was free. And I assumed I would feel free because once you're free of complications happiness should follow, that's what I thought, and now that I'd paid off a giant debt I should have felt gigantically happy. One would think. And one keeps waiting for the happiness to arrive, waiting and waiting and now here I am, remembering this apparition. She was flesh and blood, and she was friendly. And I was expecting things to be going my way, that's the expression you use when you find a penny on the ground, or a quarter, and whatever it is, if things don't go my way I can either change those things or change myself, and the mistake I made was wanting to change nothing. And I noticed that I was shivering. I wasn't cold but I was shivering. And when I leaned back in my chair she could see my shirt and the blood on my shirt and I'm fine, I said, not because I thought I was but because what's the point. What was I going to do? I imagined her laying a damp cloth on my forehead, cool and calming, and I'll see a doctor, I said, later, and for the first time in days I let my eyes close. And was the adrenaline leaving my body? I don't think so. But I was tired. When she talked to me her voice was like the cool, wet cloth, soothing, except there was no wet cloth. They talk about not closing your eyes when you're wounded, when you feel like giving up and going into what feels like sleep but it's death. That's when you're supposed to stay awake. Stay awake or die. And when I looked up there she was, and her eyes were not like my daughter's eyes. Her eyes had seen things and mine had too, we had that in common. And her lips. The adrenaline was mixing me up I guess because I thought I'd been going somewhere and now here I was, and if this was where I'd been going and where she'd been going, the question was, if there was a question, and the answer to the question, I didn't know any of it. And I didn't mind. I could almost call it peace, but distracting me from the peace was the pain. And in the confusion of all those things happening together she told me I needed to see a doctor. And the hard part was sitting up. The muscles in my back, the obliques and the obturator, they were injured, and the pain was real but I didn't say, would you give me a hand? I managed to sit upright on my own. And it felt better being upright, not great, but that's what I had to adjust to. Whatever feeling was there. And it's strange how love, the feeling we call love, is so slippery. It slips from one object to another, and we think the particular object is causing the love but now I suddenly wanted to embrace this person in front of me, a person I didn't know, but I did know her. She was my daughter and my wife, and she wasn't Rachel either but I saw Rachel and, where have you been? And it's true I'd never looked for her, never tried to find out what club or what class she was dancing in, and everything passes. As if the person in front of me is a mirror, or was, and the bleeding seemed to be slowing down, and if she was a mirror reflecting everything I knew, and as a consequence everything I was, was that a part she was playing? The jukebox song wasn't finished but I had my own part to play, and whether it was foisted on me, or whether I wanted it foisted on me, now it was out of my control. Bye-bye, I said, and when I stepped out onto the sidewalk, at that hour, in that part of town, there weren't many cabs so I walked. The moon was up there, gibbous I believe, moving westward, and I followed the moon, the pain in my side still there when I moved but now it was less intrusive. My mind could turn to other things, like the night air, cool and loud, and it was almost enjoyable, the act of walking, legs striding, arms swinging, blood flowing, but because I didn't want my blood to flow *out*, when I saw an empty taxi I hailed it.

Inside the Crazy Horse the audience sounded angry. They were booing, stomping their feet, pretending to be angry because the show hadn't started. I walked to the bar where Cosmo, standing

by the cash register, phone to his ear, was saying, the show can't
go on without you. The stage was empty except for the spotlights, red and green, and the show hadn't started because Teddy
had gone on strike. He was refusing to play his part, but the
audience loves you, Cosmo was telling him, and the girls love
you, and I sat at the bar, listening. When I nodded to Cosmo
he nodded to me, too preoccupied to notice the blood on my
shirt and I didn't tell him. I ordered a beer from Sonny, and
the problem was, the dancers had learned to perform their parts
a certain way, with Teddy, and they needed his portrayal of
Mr. Sophistication, or thought they did, to give them the freedom to be whoever they wanted to be on stage. Without a Mr.
Sophistication they refused to perform, and Cosmo, like a pantomime, was pulling at his hair. He was worried, obviously, but
when he walked up on the stage I was oddly relaxed, drinking
beer, my belly burning but only slightly, more warmth than heat,
and I imagined a cartoon animal, the liquid beer flowing out of
the bullet hole like water out of a fountain. If I sat straight, balancing my body without using my obliques, I could enjoy the
show, which at this point was Cosmo pacing the stage, holding a
microphone, improvising. He started telling jokes, and when the
jokes ran out he did a little soft shoe, buying rounds of drinks,
introducing the waitstaff, basically taking up time, killing it as
they say, and that's when I saw, at a table near the stage, a hand
waving to me. It belonged to Freddie. It was perched like a bird
on his arm, an insistent bird, calling me over, so I took a last sip
of beer, and when I got to his table he wanted me to sit. And
talk. About what happened. You're a real hero, he said. That was
some stunt. *Molto delizioso.* He thought I was Italian, or that I
spoke Italian, and when I turned to look at the stage, because

Cosmo wasn't there anymore, there was nothing to see, and our friends, Freddie said, meaning his friends, were dying to hear my story. How I did it. We didn't think you would actually . . . and I told him to tell his friends I was tired. I wasn't feeling so good. I'm not in the mood, I said, for going anywhere. Cosmo wasn't standing at his usual spot by the bar, and a few minutes later I was walking outside with Freddie.

In the story, Petrushka has already killed the Moor, but in doing so he's been injured. And the Charlatan wants to finish the job. I was sitting on a red milk crate and Freddie was leaning against his blue Chevrolet. We were back at the parking garage, but this time we'd come to the top, and under the night sky the conversation we had basically boiled down to the pros and cons of killing me. Apparently they thought I wouldn't return from Chinatown, not alive, what with the car and the bookie's bodyguards, although it turned out he wasn't a bookie, he was a Chinatown gang boss, a competitor, and what I was was a loose end, an embarrassing one but Freddie had scruples. The fact I'd held up my end of the bargain meant something. But there was also the fact that the Chinese gang would want retribution, they'd want an eye for an eye and I was supposed to be that eye, but he wasn't convinced it was right to get killed for doing your job. And I didn't want to seem to be selling him, because if he thought I was trying to cajole him or persuade him, although that's what I'd be doing, he might resist. So I went at it indirectly. I told him that logically, yes, his job was to murder me, that's what was expected of him and that's what people do, they go to work, do their jobs, but without ever thinking, like sheep, or what were those animals that were supposed to jump off cliffs? They were like lemurs, or ferrets, some kind of rodent, and their job was to act out a part and his job was the same. That's what I told him. His job wasn't to jump off a cliff but whatever it was, yes he could do it, and I said *could*, not *should* or *will* because I wanted to give him what they call wiggle room. To decide for himself. He was leaning against his car, his forearm resting on the rear windshield, and the last time we'd come to this parking lot it hadn't been good but this time we were on the top level, open to the air, the sky above me, the lights of Hollywood off to my left and the ocean, far away, to my right, and I knew the feeling of trying to *seem* relaxed, which is the opposite of *being* relaxed, and I felt the difference because I felt the gun in my pocket. I'd forgotten to wipe off my prints and throw it away and now, although I had no experience being who I was being, that's who I was. And I was nervous, but I wasn't scared. Maybe killing a person makes you not scared, I don't know, but Freddie noticed my shirt. The blood was a patch of dark red blackness below my right rib and he said, looks like you got hit. Not bad, I said, and I could feel the pistol's textured grip in my pocket. I'll get it looked at, I said, and the way he looked at me, as if he had a hearing problem, or was retarded, or maybe he was thinking about his job. Freddie, although he was supposed to kill me, was trying to figure out a way that not killing me made sense. And to help him, I told him that, although he *could* kill me, and most people probably would, some people have a code. Lemmings were the animals I was thinking of, although they don't actually jump off cliffs, and although I used the word *code*, I didn't clarify what code I was talking about, hinting at only the outline of a code, letting him fill in the details of what that code ought to be, or what *his* code ought to be, and it's not that

I convinced him of the code's morality or even the code's existence. Well, maybe I did convince him of that. The red light of the LIVE NUDE GIRLS sign was flashing down on the street, and I told him, I can disappear. No one will have to see me again. And by presenting a logical way out of a situation he'd rather not be in, he was able to get out of it. Don't think I'm letting you live, he said, because that won't happen. And then he opened the door of his blue Chevrolet, brushed off his slacks, got in, backed up, and when he drove away, although I seemed to be out of the so-called woods I wasn't.

The tragedy of Petrushka is the tragedy of us all. That's what Haskell says, but the story of Petrushka is not completely tragic. Yes, at the end of the ballet he's dead, but by dying he's freed himself from the person who controlled him, or the idea that did, and punished him, and although he's never been loved, he knows what love is. Like a Pierrot, and like any fool, he believes in the possibility of . . . and I was going to say *transformation* but it's really just possibility, which is why he seems to always return, always the same sad clown, and he never really dies because, as Haskell is trying to say, he's me.

Upstairs in the dressing room, I sat in front of a mirror, not looking at myself but there I was, or *here* I was, putting my face on. That's what my mother called it when she put her rouge and eyeliner and lipstick on. And I was using a thick, black, oil-based pencil, drawing first the outline of a mustache, the handlebar curl that spirals around my cheek and then I penciled it in, dark and slightly maniacal, but I wasn't feeling maniacal. I was calm. I was getting ready for another role, and whether it made me happy, or made happiness possible, or whether it allowed some forgetfulness to seep between the cracks that separated me from the role I had played, or roles, didn't matter. What mattered was the playing. Entering a role is like entering the ocean, like stepping in and fighting the waves to get beyond the waves, and although I couldn't play Mr. Sophistication the way Teddy played him, once I'd put the mustache on, and the red lips, and my face was painted white, like a ghost or like death, Mr. Sophistication was me. Or I was him. And they talk about *owning* the role, meaning possessing, or being possessed, and the person I saw in the mirror was not what I thought I would be, or what I'd wanted to be, but sometimes, to become who you are you have to change who you are. And I wasn't acting like him, I *was* him, Mr. Sophistication, or he was me, and the hole in the side of his back was aching. I took off the shirt I was wearing, damp with blood, dropped it in the oil-drum trash can, and the hole was still bleeding. But not badly. But I seemed to be getting sleepy, which is why I kept breathing. The painful part was getting my arms and my head through Teddy's T-shirt, the one with the bow tie printed on the front. I found it hanging on a hook, and it didn't smell bad and I didn't bother changing my pants. I put on Teddy's tuxedo coat, walked to the top of the steep stairs, and before I took the first step I remembered the top hat. It was on the shelf above Teddy's mirror, and the top hat was part of the person I was being, or going to be, and I set it on my head. I looked in the mirror, adjusting the hat, lying to myself that I looked fine and felt fine and it didn't matter because for an instant, a fairly long instant, the face I saw in the mirror wasn't my face, and what would she be like if she had lived? I would never know. And then, holding the wobbly handrail I walked down the stairs. Sherri and Darlene were down in the so-called wings, sitting on folding chairs, and I sat with them, on the last rung of the steps. They were glad I was there, I think, telling me not to worry about my lines. Just go out there, Sherri said, you'll be great. The red-haired dancer was on the opposite side of the stage, invisible to me, and Sherri and Darlene were wearing their black fishnet stockings, their lips red, and they didn't notice my T-shirt turning red, and I didn't mention it because I wanted the show to go on. I took shallow inhales because it seemed less painful, but pain was part of the job. Life means work which means playing the part, and it didn't matter if I'd never been to Vienna. You make up the place and you make up the self that resides in that place, and the art is to make it up well, to feel comfortable. And comfort is relative. I had a hole in the middle of my body, and I was feeling that hole and at the same time I was listening to Sherri and Darlene talk about what they were going to eat after the show, and I was listening to the music as it started to fade, and when the two of them stood up I also stood up, and that's when Sherri gave me a kiss. In the middle of my handlebar mustache. She wished me *merde*, and I could still smile. I wasn't that sleepy. I remembered the phrase you're supposed to respond with, *break a leg*, and I could see her thick makeup, and the sleepiness felt like a cloud, and I was under the cloud, but it wasn't raining yet. I was still breathing. And Sherri showed me where to stand, on a spot behind the middle of the curtain. She moved to her spot, next to Darlene at the side of the curtain, and like the tides of the ocean, emotion is constantly moving, flowing in or out and it's normal to be sad, and then sadness changes, like the afternoon light changes, gradually, but you feel it, even if you're not aware of it, and Sherri was limbering up, bending and twisting, and I felt stiff, but that was fine. On the other side of the curtain the crowd was clapping and booing and I heard Cosmo pull the microphone off its stand. I could feel his footsteps vibrating on the stage, not far from me but separated from me by the curtain. He was waiting for the audience, his audience, to quiet down, and they did, slowly, and he thanked them for their patience. He called them friends, Romans, then he paused. Just kidding, he said, and then he said, but seriously, folks. And when he said it, that was the cue for the music to start, the Viennese waltz, and the show that had to go on was starting, the momentum moving, and direct from the capitals of the world, he said, and the girls were peeking through a crack in the curtain, whispering to each other, and when I peeked through the curtain I saw Cosmo, his silhouette pointing to the cardboard Ringstrasse and the Ferris wheel and the house of Sigmund Freud. And then the whispering stopped. This was what they call the last minute, the moment before who I was going to be would finally appear, the moment he said, Ladies and gentlemen, it's my pleasure to give you—and here he paused, and the crowd went quiet, the ice cubes stopped tinkling, and whatever sleepiness I might have felt I fought it, and then I heard him say my name—Mr. Sophistication. That was the moment I was supposed to part the curtain, walk to the microphone, and that's when I looked to my left, to the spot where the red-haired dancer was supposed to be standing, and that's when I thought about Rachel. I'd never said good-bye to her. And it wouldn't have done any good to imagine her, standing there, because I never would say good-bye, and the ache in my lower back was everywhere. Cosmo was telling the audience, he must be delayed at the airport. And when I turned, away from whatever thoughts

I was having I saw my hands, in front of me, holding the curtain. And again Cosmo said, Ladies and gentlemen . . . Mr. Sophistication. And the hands, which were my hands, parted the curtain. The light was blinding but I stepped into it, seeing nothing but light at first, and hearing nothing, blind and deaf, but the stool was there, the microphone resting on the stool, and when I got to that, with one hand touching the stool, I looked out, letting the spotlights hit me, and the eyes of the audience, and when I sat on the edge of the stool the pain and the sleepiness, they didn't leave but now I heard clapping, *applause* would be too strong a word, but some of the people were clapping their hands, and I saw the legs of the people close to the stage, crossed over other legs, feet moving, and looking out into the darkness I was inviting whoever was out there to join me, to join me on a sentimental journey. To old Vienna. The mysterious city of cobblestones and clock towers, and once the show got started, one by one, Sherri and Darlene and whoever it, they offered to show me the Kunst Museum, and people laughed at that, and as the story proceeded they gradually removed their lederhosen and their leather jackets, and the next thing I knew, although it wasn't actually the next thing because it was all part of the same thing, the act of living my life. I was talking and gesturing, and although my brain was trying to sleep I kept my eyes, like windows, open, watching the people on stage with me, watching them dance because that's what they loved, and it's what they did. And I was listening to the music because when the music changed it would be my cue, and when I heard it change I lifted the microphone, my lips almost touching the black metal and I cleared my throat. The music was ready and the lights were ready and I began, *Falling in love again, Never wanted to,* half singing, half speaking, letting the words come out of my mouth, hearing the words as if they were made by my voice. *What was I to do.* The eyes closing, the memories fading.

Helpless.

Acknowledgments

My appreciation goes out to, among many others, Ethan and Brigid and Jackie and Barbara and Chris and Laura, Suzanne and Annie-B, and especially Athena.

JOHN HASKELL is the author of the story collection *I Am Not Jackson Pollock* and the novels *American Purgatorio* and *Out of My Skin*. His stories and essays have appeared on the radio, in anthologies, and in magazines. He is the recipient of a fellowship from the John Simon Guggenheim Foundation and has taught writing and literature in New York, Los Angeles, and Leipzig.

The text of *The Complete Ballet* is set in Adobe Caslon Pro. Book design by Rachel Holscher. Composition by Bookmobile Design and Digital Publisher Services, Minneapolis, Minnesota. Manufactured by Versa Press on acid-free, 30 percent postconsumer wastepaper.